The Best Home

Dennis E. Walsh

Table of Contents

1

A New Day in Hidden Falls

There are no wrong turnings.

Only paths we had not known we were meant to walk.

—Guy Gavriel Kay

The day seemed like any other until it didn't. Anna Halstead walked the girls, Esther and Melissa, to the bus stop down their beautiful tree-lined street and waved them off on their way to school. Back in the kitchen, she grabbed her go-cup and filled it with Peet's Dark Roast House Blend, prepared perfectly by their twelve-year-old Mr. Coffee. On the way out the door of their eighty-year-old craftsman cottage, she asked her husband, Tom, what his day was like.

"Oh, I forgot to tell you that I'm scheduled for a midmorning conference call with my boss," he said. "Not sure what it's about, but after my record-setting last quarter, I'm not too worried. Give you a shout later to update. Love you!"

On the way out to her ten-year-old minivan, she thought, *I am the luckiest girl in the world*. Two adorable daughters who were loving and precocious, a handsome and ambitious husband whom she adored, and a job that turned from "something to do" to the most fulfilling thing—outside of having children—that she had ever experienced.

Ten minutes from home, like everything else in Hidden Falls, Wisconsin, was her place of work. Serenity Acres was a chain-owned nursing home that concentrated on rural locations. Generally, they liked the labor available in these settings, meaning less expensive and for the most part very conscientious. Anna had been an ER nursing manager in Chicago before they'd moved to Hidden Falls for Tom's job. In some ways, she missed the frenetic pace and constant movement of emergency medicine in an urban environment. Gunshot wounds, construction accidents, multiple vehicle pileups, and the annual flu epidemics all made for a somewhat addictive mix of quick decisions and constant motion that many practitioners end up craving. But after a couple of years in the long-term care setting as the facility administrator, Anna grew to love Serenity Acres, its employees, its clients, and its profound impact on those who were "rounding third base," as one crotchety old member of the club told her.

Pulling through the circular drive in front of Serenity Acres, Anna took her reserved spot in the parking lot, which had room for about a hundred cars and normally only held seven or eight. The building itself was a classic midcentury U-shaped structure that had been the elementary school until about 1980, when the district consolidated into a larger entity and built a brand-new middle and elementary school complex in town. The space had been creatively adapted to long-term-care use, with classrooms subdivided into patient rooms, the cafeteria logically to a dining area, the library into a reading and game room, and the small gym into a pleasant, high-ceilinged general meeting space where all types of events took place. It wasn't perfect as a nursing home, but it was emblematic of the midwestern value of not wasting a perfectly good asset and repurposing it to something just as useful as the original intent. Serenity Acres was almost always close to full occupancy. Folks in Hidden Falls, Wisconsin, didn't move far from home when they retired or needed more care. That was viewed as "Florida flight" and associated with cites where the population was more transient. Maybe this characteristic best captured the word *heartland*.

Locking the door to the minivan, she wondered why she still carried forward that unnecessary habit after five years in Hidden Falls. Probably the decade spent in Chicago. Entering the grand entrance into the main lobby, she received the usual "Hey, boss!" from her combination receptionist, administrative assistant, director of HR, and all-around go-to person, Bonnie Freelander. The fifteen-year veteran of Serenity Acres handed her a fresh cup of Peet's and waited patiently for instructions.

"Morning, partner. Key staff all present and accounted for?" asked Anna.

"Yup. Melanie and Samantha are here, and the cook has been at it hard since 6:00, I think."

Melanie and Samantha were the two nursing managers in charge of wings A and B, respectively.

"Good. I'll check with them on staffing in a few. First, I'm headed down to breakfast to see my people. Be back in about half an hour, and we can look at the day," said Anna as she turned toward the dining room.

2

A Lovely Bunch of Coconuts!

You don't stop laughing when you grow old; you grow old when you stop laughing.

—George Bernard Shaw

Anna entered the dining room, and the smell of oatmeal, bacon, and scrambled eggs wafted over her like a warm blanket. Seated at the first table were two of her favorite residents. George Binson was a long-ago-retired landscaper who was in his late seventies and had suffered a mild right-brained hemorrhagic stroke awhile back that had impacted his impulse control but not his motor functions. June Wilhelm was, in Anna's opinion, the sweetest, most patient lady she had ever known, whom she would gladly claim as a blood relative. George gallantly offered Anna a chair and immediately asked both women a question that was indeed a novel subject for breakfast conversations.

"So I am curious, ladies. What type of erection do you two prefer? Would you be more interested in one that stood straight up and pointed to the sky, or would one that pointed right at you like a drawn pistol have more appeal?" George posed earnestly.

Anna, temporarily speechless, was saved by June's quick and perfectly calm response. "Well, George, I can't say that I have recently given much thought to that particular subject, but since you ask, I'll venture a reply. If I were interested in utilizing it as the Lord had intended—which I am not—I suppose that either version would be satisfactory. Creatively, I would prefer the fully engorged stand-on-end type so that it could be used as a coat hook for my favorite melton red winter coat with lambs'-wool collar. It's rather heavy, don't you see?" Glancing at Anna calmly, June winked and waited for George to process her suggestions.

After the longest ten seconds that Anna had ever experienced, George said, "Splendid! Did either of you notice the crocuses coming up at the entrance this morning? It's the earliest I can ever recall seeing them showing."

Rising, Anna said, "I'll check them out, George, and you two enjoy your breakfasts. That bacon smells yummy!" In making her exit, Anna thought, *you just can't make that shit up! Love this place.*

Walking away from the table with the indelible image of George gallantly supporting June's good winter coat from his excited member embedded in her head, Anna made her way toward the middle of the dining room, where the Vera Bradley Bridge Mafia was chatting over coffee. The group consisted of the four leading matriarchs of Hidden Valley, each from a prominent family. Their leader by mutual understanding was Emmaline Yoder, the head of the Yoder agricultural empire that consisted of a two thousand–acre dairy farm, a famous cheese manufacturing plant known nationwide, and vast real estate holdings. The second member was Sarah Wilson, whose family owned and operated the First Farmers Trust Bank, headquartered in Hidden Falls with fifteen branch locations across central Wisconsin. Member number three was Verna Winstadt, whose late husband had started and grown the Winstadt Group into one of the largest independent insurance agencies in the Midwest, specializing in property casualty for commercial clients. Last but not least was Suzanne Richards Holmby, the owner and past editor of the *Hidden Falls Chronicle*, Wisconsin's last independently run newspaper.

As Anna approached the table, she heard Emmaline ask Suzanne, "Why in God's name didn't you bid two clubs based on what I had opened?"

Suzanne calmly finished chewing her small bite of danish and responded, "Emma dear, I'm not really sure why I committed such a grievous error, but I am confident that if there is a God, he really doesn't give a good healthy crap about our bridge game."

Emmaline smiled and chuckled before she looked up to acknowledge Anna by asking her if she could fetch them all some more coffee. A few years ago, that type of request might have irritated Anna a bit, but not anymore. She knew exactly who she worked for, and it wasn't the headquarters outside of Philadelphia, nine hundred–plus miles away. It was the four beautiful ladies seated at the table and the rest of those enjoying breakfast.

Consequently, she replied, "You bet, Emmaline. Be right back."

She walked over to the kitchen window opening and asked Cookie (a.k.a. Doreen Klemposki) for a refill on the pot. Doreen promptly filled it from the industrial-sized coffee maker in the kitchen and handed it back, asking if the Mafia was bitching about breakfast or the service.

"Not at all," replied Anna. "They were just making sure I still remember who runs the place. And by the way, can I get a plate of scrambled eggs with one slice of bacon and a danish to take back to my office if I promise to bring the plate back?"

"You got it, boss," called Cookie.

Anna made her way back down the hall to her office with her breakfast, which was working hard on her salivary glands.

Bonnie poked her head around the corner and told her that both Melanie and Samantha wanted to talk about the same issue when she had a minute.

"Now is as good a time as any," Anna said.

3

A More Enlightened Approach

Friendship is a wildly underrated medication.

—Anna Deavere Smith

Melanie Grogan Smith and Samantha Smith Grogan were the two best hires Anna had made since coming to Serenity Acres. They were a married couple that met in nursing school ten years back and had been instantly attracted to each other. Their interests, tastes, senses of humor, and values were mirrored in the other. They were wed after their graduation from the nursing program at Indiana University Medical Center in Indianapolis, at which time they started their master's degrees in nursing, specializing in geriatric medicine. Karma had smiled on Anna when she posted two nurse manager openings three years ago and received their résumés on the same day. A week later, they showed up together for their interviews, and Anna had immediately extended offers, which they had instantly accepted. For the last three years, Melanie and Samantha had organized the nursing function at Serenity Acres, hired LPNs and home health aides, and worked tirelessly to maintain quality standards and a happy and safe environment for their residents. The trust that had developed between the two and Anna was strong and virtually unbreakable.

Anna had a mouthful of danish when her two nurse managers showed up, so she just motioned for them to sit in the visitor chairs facing her desk. Swallowing her bite, she asked, "So how is it going, and what is the common issue you guys have that we need to discuss?"

Samantha answered the first part. "We had the usual all-staff meeting first thing this morning, and with the exception of the normal resident disagreements and schedule shifting, everything is copacetic. Don't you think, Mel?"

"Yup. On the whole, doing very well. Which brings us to the reason we wanted to meet," Melanie replied.

Anna waited, and somewhat reluctantly, Melanie continued, "I think you know us well enough by now to know that neither of us are in the habit of second-guessing medical decisions made by attending physicians of our residents. That being said, we both have new residents in our respective wings that arrived with 'interesting' orders for newly prescribed SSRIs."

That immediately piqued Anna's interest, as one of her primary goals since arriving was to closely monitor and control the use of psychotropic medications among the resident population. "OK, you know you have my attention now, guys. Elaborate."

Feeling free to speak her mind, Samantha continued, "As you know, when putting someone on any antidepressant, especially older patients, blood work is important to determine both appropriateness and dosage. Neither of us can find any evidence of that being done in our respective residents. With the normal metabolic changes in both kidney and liver functions occurring in older patients, knowing what those blood values are is not a luxury—it's a necessity. Secondly, from our experience, the initial dosing orders of 15 mg daily of Lexapro feels a bit high, especially minus the blood work. If either liver or kidney function is subnormal, that kind of dose could easily lead to too much active ingredient in their systems and thus complications. Worries us both more than a little, so we were wondering if you could check with the practice to verify."

So there it was—the ask. Anna smiled and said, "OK, I get it, and I am glad to run point on this. Well, *glad* may be an overstatement, but nonetheless, I will call over today or first thing tomorrow morning and check in with the new primary care doctor. Any idea on a name?"

Melanie chuckled and said, "Yeah, I think it's MacDonald, as in Ol' MacDonald liked his pharm."

"Oh, now that's rich and would be very funny were it not such a serious topic. You two get back to work!" Anna laughed.

*

Anna took a deep breath and decided to do some paperwork, provided generously by the state of Wisconsin in the form of the written portion of the annual quality survey, just to get her mind off the call to Dr. MacDonald who loved the pharm, e-i-e-i-o. Damn those two smart alecks, anyway. That got her through lunch, and upon her return, Bonnie handed her a note from Tom that read, "Give me a call when you get a moment. My conference call subject was interesting." Knowing her husband's penchant for understatement, she had a gut feeling she was in for another fun surprise. She decided to wait until she got home to face the music with a moderately priced glass of Napa cab.

4

Meanwhile, Back in Chicago

Ever has it been that love knows not its own depth until the hour of separation.

—Khalil Gibran

Dr. Angela Washington, the medical director of Northwestern's emergency room, was an expert at catastrophes. That was the world she lived in six days a week for roughly seventy-two action-packed hours. From "unstoppable" nosebleeds, to myocardial infarctions slight and massive, to grotesque compound fractures, to GSWs of every caliber and severity, she calmly oversaw a team that handled well in excess of eighty thousand cases annually. In other words, she lived in the equivalent of a war zone and coped with grace, humor, and incredible stamina.

Not being able to handle or address a problem was foreign to her experience, especially one so very personal. Her father had lost his beloved wife of fifty-five years and had spiraled into a blue funk that almost surely qualified as clinical depression. He had not left his house for six weeks and showed no desire to break the pattern. Angela was shocked that this incredible man could be so broken by a single event, albeit a horrific one.

Dr. Elijah Roosevelt Washington was a legend within the Chicago medical community, but he was not born to it. His father and mother were Asa Douglas Washington and Sophie Jones Washington, who worked their way up to middle-class blacks from the South Side of Chicago. Asa was a high school graduate and capable of far more had he been afforded the chance. To his credit and good fortune, he went to work for the Pullman Company and over a long career worked up through the ranks to become a supervisor of porters and a high-ranking official in the Brotherhood of Sleeping Car Porters, one of the most powerful African American political entities of the early twentieth century. Asa and Sophie's house was filled with books, art, and music, to which Elijah was introduced at a very early age. Sophie taught Elijah to play on their upright piano, and by the time he was six, he was playing by ear many of the classics as well as jazz. Asa was a self-taught fluent Latin reader and speaker, which he passed on to Elijah, convinced that it was a key building block to a sharp intellect. Their friends and neighbors on the South Side were owners of small businesses serving the community, and they all shared a common goal of raising their children to reap the promise and riches offered by the economic boom of midcentury postwar America. Depending on the day, Elijah believed his only-child status was either a blessing or a curse.

A turning point in young Elijah's life was the opportunity presented by one of his father's white customers who traveled extensively on the Pullman cars. This successful businessman was on the board of the Latin School of Chicago and offered to get Elijah an interview with the director of admissions. His mastery of Latin and his musical skills landed him a full scholarship, and he spent grades five through twelve happily at Chicago Latin, where he ran track, swam, and won numerous academic awards. Many of his classmates went on to leadership positions in the private sector and government in Chicago. Elijah's aptitude for math and the sciences landed him once again on scholarship at the University of Chicago, where he completed his undergrad degree in three years and most importantly met his beautiful wife, Sandra Hargrave. She hailed from the "exotic" city of St. Louis and was universally recognized as a breathtaking beauty who was majoring in marketing. Following the wedding, Elijah was off to the Pritzker

School of Medicine, and Sandra was hired as an assistant buyer at Marshall Field's.

They starved through his med school years and residency on Sandra's salary at Field's—though it grew slightly with promotions—mandating a steady diet of beans and rice, love for each other, and a bunch of friends in the same boat. In the end, there they were, broke and happy, with the world at their fingertips. Offers poured in for Elijah after completion of his residency at Northwestern with a specialty in internal medicine. For the first time in his life, his race was a real upside. Many major hospital systems were eagerly seeking highly qualified black candidates to join their teams and build more diverse medical staffs. After offers from Mayo, the Cleveland Clinic, Henry Ford, Barnes-Jewish, and Northwestern Memorial, Elijah was drawn to his hometown. The food, the jazz clubs, the sports teams, and the general aura of the Windy City had a grip on him that was born in a deep feeling of belonging. And so a distinguished career of service and commitment at Northwestern Memorial began in the mid-'70s for Dr. Elijah Roosevelt Washington followed by the birth of their only child, Angela, in 1980.

So now, the daughter who idolized her dad and followed him into medicine was driving out to her parents' house in Oak Park to check on "the man." He who had been the barrier-breaking, brilliant, compassionate healer his whole professional life was now in need of healing, and she felt woefully inadequate to the task. She pulled under the porte cochere of her parents' 1913 Frank Lloyd Wright–designed and –built house and walked up the steps to the massive wooden front door with stained glass. The structure was a low-slung redbrick affair that most people found amazing. Such is the work of genius. She took out her key and quietly opened the huge door. Leaving the two-story front entry hall, she made her way to the study, where she found her dad sitting in his leather reading chair and staring straight ahead at nothing. He was wrapped in the Restoration Hardware bathrobe she had given him the previous Christmas, and he wore a pair of Ralph Lauren flannel lounging pants in a black watch pattern with a black T-shirt. Even in his current condition, he was a stylish picture. The closet in the master bedroom housed over forty English bespoke suits and sport coats from his favorite tailor on Carnaby Street in London. She was pretty sure the twenty pounds he had dropped since her mother passed would make them hang rather loosely on his six-foot-three frame.

She stood in front of him and asked, "So what have you had to eat today?"

He pointed to the kitchen as if to say, *Go check for yourself.*

Angela navigated the hallway to the front of the house and walked into the large open kitchen. On the middle island was a box from the neighborhood Whole Foods that had been delivered by their parent company, Amazon, the day before. She grabbed the packing slip and read: granola, 1 percent milk, frozen organic chicken tenders, orange juice, and Peet's Dark Roast House Blend. She checked the refrigerator and found all those things inside unopened.

Walking back to the study, she asked her dad, "Do you always refrigerate your granola?" He looked at her with the same blank stare and shrugged. *What the hell am I going to do with this guy?* Anna thought. As if by magic, the coffee had made her think of Anna Halstead, the best ER nurse manager she'd had ever had, who'd moved to Wisconsin and was now managing a well-regarded nursing home. Looking at the ceiling, Angela quietly exclaimed, "Thank you, Jesus!"

5

Make That a Bottle of Napa Cab

The pessimist complains about the wind; the optimist expects it to change; the realist adjusts the sails.

—William Arthur Ward

After delaying the call to Dr. Ian MacDonald for as long as possible with nonurgent administrative tasks, Anna looked up to see Bonnie leaning in her doorway with a sticky note. She walked over and put it in the middle of Anna's desk, closed the door, and left quietly. There in front of her was the good doctor's phone number. Sometimes her job resembled a *M*A*S*H* rerun, with Bonnie replacing Gary Burghoff.

Punching in the seven digits took about three seconds, and waiting for someone to pick up took almost three minutes, but who was counting? Finally, an overworked and short-of-breath woman announced that she had reached Dr. MacDonald's office and asked what the nature of the call was. Anna, in her friendliest and most charming voice, introduced herself as the administrator of Serenity Acres and then stated that the nature of the business was two newly admitted patients that were under Dr. MacDonald's care.

"Let me see if he has time to talk," the woman replied impatiently.

Anna listened to a country singer slaughter "Strangers in the Night" until the nurse came back on and told her that the doctor would prefer she e-mail her with the question. Anna managed a deep cleansing breath before suggesting to the nurse that doing it that way was probably not HIPAA compliant and she really would like a callback from Dr. MacDonald when he got a chance. The nurse agreed and hung up rather abruptly. *Wow, that sounds like a fun place to work*, thought Anna.

After the call, she hosted a tour of the facility for a nice couple who were considering a place for one of their mothers, who lived about twenty-five minutes away and was increasingly dependent on them for pretty much everything. While doing some selling with the help of staff and multiple residents, Anna spent most of the visit assuring them they weren't uncaring and ungrateful children who didn't have time for Mom anymore. Appreciative and feeling a bit less guilty, they exited with a commitment to get back to her by the end of the week. That was another reason she loved this job so much; caring for an aging person is an emotional event that most people are unfamiliar with and ill prepared to handle. If she could help even a little, it was gratifying.

At 4:00, the landline on her desk lit up, and Bonnie told it was Dr. MacDonald for her. After cleansing breath number two of the day, Anna said, "Dr. MacDonald, thanks so much for getting back to me, and I look forward to meeting you in person."

After a dramatic pause, Dr. MacDonald replied, "I'm not sure that is going to happen anytime soon. What can I do for you?"

Anna thought for a moment and said, "Great. I like a guy who gets right down to business. You admitted two patients last week to our facility with new prescriptions for Lexapro. We have not received any blood work on either. Our best practice calls for an evaluation. We use the Geriatric Depression Scale short form, which we have administered by our contract psychologist. Once we get those results, usually the same day as the test, we send them to the attending physician's office and make a recommendation. Depending upon the depression severity, we normally start with cognitive behavioral therapy (CBT) alone or, if merited, in combination with an antidepressant. The blood work is important because, as you know, elderly patients' metabolisms are quite different, especially in terms of renal and hepatic functions. This needs to be taken into account in dosages—initial and ongoing. This may be a little different from what you are used to, but it has worked well for us and for your predecessor. We're all looking forward to working with you and doing the best for your patients."

After another short pause, Dr. MacDonald said coldly, "Quite frankly, Ms. Halstead, I'm not used to being second-guessed by a nursing home manager."

Anna thought for a moment and then offered, "Doctor, I'm not second-guessing you. I'm simply sharing how we operate here. Furthermore, I am a master's-degreed nurse by training, my two nurse managers have master's degrees with geriatric specialties, and the facility has an immaculate record in psychotropic mediation management as witness to our state survey scores. So are we going to work together to take care of your patients?"

"My office will be in touch," barked the doctor, who then clicked off abruptly.

Anna smiled and thought; *I guess every town needs a few pompous assholes.*

She cleared her desk, grabbed her Kate Spade bag, and told Bonnie, "Put a fork in me, partner. I'm done for the day."

"See you in the morning, boss. I will expect the lowdown on your initial call with our new doctor," said Bonnie.

*

Anna could not remember when she had been looking forward to a glass of wine more than she was during the short drive home. She pulled in the driveway, slammed the door of her "vintage" minivan, and climbed the front steps of their beloved cottage. She opened the door to find Tom sitting in the living room with two stemless wineglasses and a bottle of 2015 Caymus cab.

She smiled, looked at him, and said, "OK. We have three possible explanations for this extravagance. One, I forgot our anniversary. Two, you are having an affair with a coworker. Three, your conference call with your boss was good news."

Tom laughed and said, "Let's go for door number three."

She handed him back her glass and quipped, "Top me off, big boy, and spill the beans. And by the way, where are the girls?"

Tom dutifully enriched his original pour and told her that the girls were in the backyard playing with two surprise gifts he was sure would buy them enough time to chat.

"Smart move. Now talk," Anna said, seating herself in her favorite armchair.

Tom sat back and started what was obviously a well-rehearsed overview of his conference call with his boss. "So my call with Ron started out pretty normal, with an update of the current quarter and some plans for this year's American Academy of Orthopedic Surgeons meeting, which, by the way, I am attending. Then he had some really nice things to say about my first-quarter performance—which, as I have told you about ten times, landed me on the top sales nationally. He said it was incredible based on the size of my region compared to some of the huge metro areas. Ron said that the other zone vice presidents were still trying to figure out how that many hips, knees, and ankles could be replaced in a state that is primarily rural. Then he reminded them that it is all about market share and that they might be giving up too much of theirs to the competition. Then he circled back to my journey over the last five years and how I had taken a weak region and, through hard work and great relationships with the major orthopedic surgeons, turned it into a winner.

"Then it got interesting. Without me knowing, the company had been tracking all the new hires that had started out over the last two years by shadowing me for a week. I know you remember me complaining that if I had wanted to babysit all day, I would have become a stay-at-home dad. Apparently, not one of these twelve reps have washed out, which is an outlier statistically for newbies. Additionally, HR surveyed all of them, and when asked to what they attributed their early success, the second or first reason was the early time spent with me. They went on to state that my advice on building relationships with surgeons in my region and my competence on the surgical process itself made each want to perfect those skills themselves. Then came the real reason for the call. Styker's current national director of sales training is retiring in August, so they want me to come to Kalamazoo next week and interview for the job. Ron says he knows who the other two internal candidates are, and he is very confident that I am the strongest choice. Lastly, the starting salary for director-level jobs is more than twice my base, and I would likely be offered close to the midpoint, which could double my income. Oh, and director-level jobs come with stock options.

I feel like a jackass. I have been talking nonstop for what feels like fifteen minutes and just realized you have tears in your eyes. I know how much you and the girls love it here, and if you want to stay, I will call Ron tonight and tell him it's a no-go."

Anna reached into her purse, grabbed a tissue, and swabbed both eyes. "Tom, you are not a jackass; you are a dumb shit. You can't even tell the difference between sad tears and joyful ones. *Men!* Right now, I am so proud of you I could pop! Get your handsome butt over here and kiss me." After another large pour of Caymus, they made their way to the kitchen, pulled the Home Chef ingredients from the refrigerator, and called the girls in from outside to start the mise en place as a family.

Before turning in for the evening, Anna shot off a quick e-mail to her boss in Chicago, Bob Struttmeir, AVP of the Upper Midwest for Silver Age Industries, asking for a quick call the next day. That was going to be an interesting conversation.

6

An Expected Fork in the Road

The only way that we can live is if we grow. The only way that we can grow is if we change. The only way that we can change is if we learn. The only way that we can learn is if we are exposed. And the only way that we can become exposed is if we throw ourselves out into the open. Do it. Throw yourself.

—C. JoyBell C.

Bob Struttmeir was in his normal spot at 7:30 in the morning—stuck in traffic on 294 headed south from his house in Deerfield to Des Plaines, where the regional office of Silver Age Industries was currently located. The ride was slightly less annoying due to his E-Class Mercedes with the custom Illinois plates that read STRUTT VP. While the car might have been enough of a message for most, Bob preferred to punctuate the point with authority and the vanity plate. *It's only vanity if it's not true,* he thought. Activating his Bluetooth phone app, he speed-dialed Anna, from whom he'd received a somewhat cryptic e-mail the night before.

Hope she's not going to shit on my day, he thought as opposed to hoping that everything was OK with her. That was just the way Bob rolled.

Anna picked up her cell, knowing it was Bob. She really liked the database's contact feature because it gave her a moment to calibrate her listening and responses based who was on the other end. After putting her mind at DEFCON 3, she proceeded. "Hey, Bob. Thanks for getting back to me so quickly. How is your day so far?" Anna chirped in her friendliest tone.

Bob replied, "Traffic sucks as usual, and Cherise committed us to a charity function at the club tonight, which means overbidding on something she wants and I don't care about, followed by a large babysitting tab. So what's up?"

Anna was momentarily thankful he was just her boss and not her spouse, but then she remembered she was not that dumb or desperate. She responded, "Well, I learned about something last night that could impact my job, and I thought I should give you a heads-up seeing as how you are just about the best boss I have ever had." There was a slight pause, which gave Anna time to stop herself from throwing up in her mouth for lying so skillfully.

Finally, Mr. Wonderful queried, "So tell me how you are going to ruin my day."

"Although we haven't talked about it much over the five years I've worked for you, Tom, my husband, works for Stryker Medical and is quite successful in his territory. Actually, he is number one nationally right now. His boss has asked him to go to Kalamazoo next week and interview for the director of sales training position, which will be open in about ninety days, and if successful, it would require a move to the corporate office."

Knowing Bob as well as she did, she wasn't sure if someone else's success or having to deal with an opening would be more troubling to him. She didn't have to wait long to find out.

"Jesus H. Christ, do you know how long it took us to fill your role the last time? Six goddamn months! It's not easy to find someone who is willing to move to the boonies" Bob exclaimed. Trying hard not to display her joy at his discomfort too openly, Anna waited for the next question. "Crap! So what are his odds of landing the job?"

Should I make them longer than they really are and prolong the prick's agony or give it to him straight and force him to pull on his big-boy pants right now? she wondered. "Well, Bob, based on what his boss said, it appears it's his job to lose, and let's just say I wouldn't bet against him."

Groaning like a petulant child, he asked, "So what should we do?"

"Good question. Here is how I see it. First, I confirm to you by the middle of next week whether it's a go or no-go. If it's a go, I immediately contact my person at Med List, the online recruiter we used to land Melanie and Samantha, our two top-drawer nurse managers." She was about 95 percent sure he had no idea who Mel and Sam were. "I'll send them the job description and preferred qualifications and have them post it immediately. It's early May, and I won't have to move the girls until mid-August, which gives us about ninety days. If you would like, I can do the initial screens and pass on viable candidates to corporate HR, who could pass on finalists to you for final interviews and an offer. I will do whatever you think best," Anna posed.

"Yeah, that all sounds OK, short of you staying at Serenity Acres, which I know is not an option. Keep me posted as soon as you know the outcome," Bob snapped and then suddenly clicked off.

Yup, thought Anna, *that's old It's-All-About-Me Bob*. He would be a great fit for the current administration in Washington. Under qualified, pretty much clueless, and so self-absorbed that he used the word *I* more than one would think humanly possible. *Well, that was fun*, she thought as she pulled into the parking lot at Serenity Acres.

7

Sometimes a Problem Can Be the Solution

If laughter is universally viewed as the best medicine, why are comedians the only ones constantly on the lookout for more things to laugh about?

—Anonymous

Despite herself, Anna's main thoughts on her way to work were the very real potential of her leaving and the resultant vacancy at Serenity Acres. She wasn't delusional in thinking that she was the only one who could do the job the way it needed to be done. Her last boss had taught her that if she did her job well, exiting should have the same effect as removing one's hand from a bucket of sand; others will fill in to maintain the organization's success and vibrancy because of one's mentoring and management. The issue was getting someone who would fit with the team to come live in Hidden Falls. Bob's description of the town was certainly inaccurate, but having said that, finding someone with the requisite qualifications willing to move there was not going to be easy. It didn't matter. She was going to make it happen if necessary.

Oddly, when she walked into the facility and checked in with Bonnie, Bonnie handed her a note saying that a Dr. Angela Washington had called and asked that she return the call posthaste. Now that was weird or at least something cosmic, as she had been thinking about her just three minutes earlier. She closed her door and immediately called Angela as requested. Angela picked up on her cell, and Anna heard the sounds of the ER in the background as Angela said, "Oh, thank God, it's you! Let me walk outside for some privacy. OK, I feel a little bad we haven't talked in some time, and here I am calling you for a humongous favor, but here it goes. My mom passed very unexpectedly about six weeks ago, and it has hit my dad like a ton of bricks. He has not left the house, and I'm pretty sure he is existing on Peet's dark roast and maybe five hundred calories of either granola or chicken a day. He is losing weight, uncommunicative, quiet, and sedentary, which all point to clinical depression. My world hasn't slowed down one bit and isn't going to anytime soon. Knowing him as I know him, if I try to bring someone in, he will either eat them alive or just retreat further into his blue funk. I know you are running one of the best long-term-care facilities in the state of Wisconsin, which is about a three-hour drive from here. I'm confident that Dad can come out of this, but he needs help, and I'm not the one to deliver it. Anna, I'm desperate, scared, and unsure what to do."

Her voice trailed off, and Anna said, "Angela, do you remember what I told you when I left five years ago?"

"To be honest, not word for word," replied Angela.

"Not to worry; I do. I told you that you were the best boss I had ever had, that you were an inspiration to every woman working at Northwestern, that I would miss you terribly, and, lastly, that if I could ever do anything for you to call me immediately. So to my way of thinking, you are just following instructions. When can you have him here? We have a wing that is populated with a mix of LTC patients and assisted-living residents who need some help that would be a great environment for him. There is a room available, and the day he arrives, we will have our psychologist run him through the geriatric depression scale and put together a treatment plan. What do you think?"

Angela answered with equal measures of relief and emotion, "Is tomorrow OK? I can take the day, drive him up, and probably be there by midafternoon."

Without hesitation, Anna said, "Can't wait to see you, boss, and to welcome your father. It will be an honor to have him here, and we will get him back on his feet. Lastly, I have to share that I thought of you this morning and something you told me about nobody being indispensable, and it helped me immensely. Weird, don't you think?"

With brightness back in her voice, Angela said, "Even weirder when you realize that my dad is the one who shared that bit of wisdom with me. We will both see you tomorrow afternoon. Love you, Anna."

"Back at you, Angela. Safe travels." Anna smiled in response.

*

Anna headed back to her office and hunkered down with the door closed to put together a modified Gantt chart that outlined a transition plan for Serenity Acres to new leadership. It included each department reviewing their performance improvement plans and updating them if called for, a review of all employee appraisals, and a mandate for a formal presentation about their respective departments. It also included an action plan for the recruitment of her replacement that she had briefly outlined for the Struttmeister. She finished this and turned to the regular business of the day until about 11:45 when she felt like she owed herself a break, so she headed for the dining room to mingle with "her people," as she fondly thought of them.

After checking in with Cookie and her staff, she asked where the Vera Bradley Bridge Mafia was hiding. Cookie said that they were taking their lunch under one of the umbrella tables in the courtyard and that she had heard quite a bit of laughter about fifteen minutes earlier. Anna thanked her and wound her way through the dining room, making inquiries about everyone's lunch and news of the day. After about ten more minutes, she exited the french doors into the courtyard and saw the group seated with cards in hand at a table up against George's rose garden, which was coming to life earlier than usual. Anna walked up, noticing the pitcher of "lemonade," and inquired how they were and what had been so funny earlier. That started another full minute of tearful laughing by the group. When they caught their breaths and dried their eyes, they all looked to Suzanne, the newspaper baron, to explain.

Suzanne collected herself and started, "Well, it really was precipitated by Emmaline's insistence that we have several pitchers of Leinenkugel Summer Shandy with our lunch, even knowing that it gave Verna the 'wind,' as she delicately puts it. Well, about three hands into our game, Verna let loose with a prolonged burst that Sarah later said was louder than her father's 1936 Hudson backfiring. There was a bit of dignified mouth-covered chuckling until that crazy George Binson, who was weeding just over there in the roses, jumped up and screamed at the top of his lungs, 'Fire in the hole! Fire in the hole!' Needless to say, that set off a full ten-minute laugh fest that probably caused us to collectively consume four full Kleenex purse packages. After we finally got back in control of ourselves and Emma admitted she had probably wet herself a bit, I explained the origin of the phrase *fire in the hole,* stating that it was shouted when coal miners set off a major explosion in an enclosed space. Well, that started the whole laughing thing again. I think we are all pretty exhausted from the effort. Does that cover it, girls?"

"Yes, Suzanne dear, and could we please move off the topic and on to something more enlightening and ladylike?" pleaded Verna.

That little vignette pretty much represented what the place meant to Anna. Friendship, laughter, and a warm, safe environment created to allow anyone who came to stay the best home possible. She was going to work hard to keep it going.

8

Taking the High Road

The one thing you can say about the high road, there doesn't seem to be a lot of traffic on it these days.

—Randy Vader

The next morning when Anna pulled into her reserved space in the nearly empty parking lot, she noticed a new Audi A8 in a visitor's space about five slots down. She appraised the young man in the driver's seat busily thumbing out a message on his iPhone, thought she knew who it was, and proceeded inside. Passing Bonnie, Anna told her that she would be in her office and had a feeling that Dr. MacDonald was going to be entering shortly and to come get her immediately when he checked in. After about ten minutes, which gave her time to finish her mugful of coffee and mentally review her to-do items for the day, Bonnie was at the door announcing the arrival of Dr. MacDonald, followed by a not-to-subtle wink.

Anna walked out of her office to greet a moderately tall and nice-looking midthirties guy who looked her square in the eye with no emotion whatsoever. She waved him into her office, and thinking quickly, she said, "So you were the guy sitting in the new Audi A8 outside giving someone instructions on your iPhone. Tell me, does the V6 Turbo have the acceleration they claim?"

Dr. MacDonald thought for a few seconds and then smiled in spite of himself and replied, "Yeah, it's quick, and I have to watch myself. I love accelerating way faster than I really need to."

"OK. Let me just clear the air. I hope our first conversation regarding your two patients didn't give the impression that I believe my judgment or knowledge concerning their condition or care is greater than yours. I have worked successfully with doctors my entire career in health care and have nothing but respect for their skills and dedication. In case you didn't notice, my passion for taking care of those entrusted to us sometimes gets the best of me. My dad used to tell me that when that happened, I was letting my mouth overload my ability to cash the check. So do you think we could start over?" Anna offered.

Dr. MacDonald looked squarely at her and then stated, "If we are clearing the air, let me start by confessing that taking over this practice from someone who had run it successfully for forty years is a bit more daunting than I'd imagined. I'm pretty sure I came across as a pompous prick during our first exchange, and it would be great if you could give me a second chance. And by the way, call me Ian."

Anna gave a nice long exhalation and then said, "Great! So where would you like to start, Ian?"

"You know the ropes around here far better than I do, Anna. Walk me through it."

"Pretty straightforward with a few moving parts. Let's start by getting our phlebotomist from the hospital lab out here this afternoon and drawing blood on both. The lab at the hospital can have us the results by tomorrow. Then we have our psychologist run the GDS short form and get the results to us. We need orders from you on that and the blood work. So realistically, in a couple of days, we can talk, and you can decide on Lexapro alone, Lexapro with a standard cognitive behavioral therapy routine attached, or just cognitive behavioral therapy as a stand-alone approach."

"How long have you been doing this, Anna?" asked Ian sheepishly.

"Just about five years, and I've almost got the hang of it," said Anna.

"Let me go get my script pad out of the car—and there is no doubt: I was a pompous prick," Ian offered as he walked away.

*

Approximately 230 miles southeast of Hidden Falls, Dr. Angela Washington and her father were finally seated comfortably in her Porsche Cayenne, heading north toward Hidden Falls and Serenity Acres. Her decision to go over the night before and pack one of the large roller bags used for European travel with a multiple-week supply of Elijah's casual clothes and the necessary toiletries had been wise. She didn't bother to inform him what she was doing upstairs in the master bedroom and left afterward, saying she would see him in the morning. After getting him into some travel togs—an Armani sweat suit—and pointing the speedy SUV northwest against the flow of traffic, she tuned in some progressive jazz and drove. Fifteen minutes into the journey, her father asked where the hell they were headed. Angela hesitated and then decided that even in his altered state, he was not someone you could bullshit.

"I'm taking you up to a friend's health-care facility in midstate Wisconsin to recuperate from the shock of Mom's death. You are not eating, exercising, reading, or doing anything productive. Frankly, I think you are depressed, and I can't devote the time to get you back on your feet, and that's what they do where we are headed. That's the long and short of it, Elijah."

"Mind your manners, young lady, with the use of my given name," he chided without looking at her.

Nothing else was said until they arrived in Hidden Falls at Serenity Acres two hours and forty minutes later.

9

Feeling Like a Stranger in a Strange Land

There is no safety this side of the grave.

—Robert A. Heinlein

Elijah's arrival and early days at Serenity Acres reinforced lessons that Anna had learned in her eight years in emergency room medicine. Trauma, whether to the physical body, the mind, or emotions, is not something that is cured overnight despite all the advances in modern medicine. The staff had collectively decided to give Elijah space for first couple of days, and he had chosen to remain in his room, which is exactly what Angela had predicted. On day two of his stay, Anna had arranged for Dr. Penelope Lipscombe, their contract psychologist, to come for an initial assessment and to run Dr. Washington through the GDS as planned. Not surprisingly, he had scored a twenty-five, which indicated severe clinical depression. Dr. Lipscombe had inserted the results into Elijah's chart and gave Anna, Melanie, Samantha, and Dr. MacDonald a heads-up. They all agreed that cognitive behavioral therapy (talk therapy, in layman's terms) would be the primary course of treatment with a mild dosage of the antidepressant Lexapro to assist the process. Dr. Washington, asserting himself for the first time—a healthy sign—refused the antidepressant, which was always honored when a patient was deemed competent, as was this case. So the first session of therapy was scheduled for early the following week, and all agreed a close watch on his food consumption, communication with staff, and activity and mobility would be the initial step. The good news was that Cookie's skills in the facility kitchen were beginning to pay off with clean plates of food being removed from Elijah's room three times per day. Small steps were needed before someone willingly got back into the game.

If everything was normal and boring inside Dr. Washington's room in B wing of Serenity Acres, the exact opposite had been the case in the rest of the facility since his arrival. While all the residents of the facility had certainly seen and even conversed with black people in the past, few if any had ever lived with one. Their exposure was primarily a product of trips to either Milwaukee or Chicago to go shopping or to attend a sporting event. In one case, most of the participants on the field or court were indeed black, and in the other, stores were definitely populated with integrated workforces for decades. For Serenity Acre's inhabitants, cohabitation with someone of a different race evoked excited curiosity, outright fear, or barely subdued rage. The net effect was a continuous walker and wheelchair parade that snaked down B wing in nonstop fashion. Getting a glimpse of the new inhabitant in one of the assisted suites was the rough equivalent of a Sasquatch sighting the first couple of days after his arrival. The rumors of who he was, why he was there, and what it would do to Serenity's reputation were rampant. The *who* part had the most creative answers of the three questions. There was speculation he was the exiled leader of an African nation who had fifteen wives. Another account had him as a former NBA All-Star and color TV analyst. The favorite had him as a famous jazz saxophonist who had toured with the big bands in his youth. The reasons for his admittance were neatly compacted into either drug habit, PTSD-related problems, or eating disorder categories. For the residents, it was better fodder for gossip than if Bonnie had been revealed as a mob wife in witness protection.

The staff was pleased that, for many of the residents, it was the most unforced exercise they had experienced in years. While the ultimate goal was to get Dr. Washington up and moving around, there were obvious benefits to the resident population due to his cloistered situation that the staff appreciated.

The other big news came from Melanie and Samantha. Anna feared when they asked for another private meeting that they were moving, which she didn't even want to think about in the face of her potential departure. The real reason was something that would probably in fact anchor them to Hidden Falls for years to come. They had decided to have a baby. The first step was to research sperm banks in the Midwest and develop a profile of the donor they would like. Anna was delighted for them and was fairly certain she had found a topic of conversation and speculation among the resident population that might even eclipse the new resident in B wing.

10

A Change It Gonna Come

Every next level of your life will demand a different you.

—Leonardo DiCaprio

On Tuesday of the following week, Anna got a call from Tom, who had traveled on Monday to Kalamazoo for his interview at the Stryker headquarters. It was one of those moments when she knew what she was likely to hear and hoped she had prepared to respond as the best version of herself. She took the call in her office, and she could tell immediately by the energy in her husband's voice what she would hear next.

"Hi, sweetheart! I just finished with the COO, which was a real surprise. She isn't normally in the interview rotation for director-level jobs. After about five minutes, I had a feeling where the conversation was headed because her questions were more about my view of the company and my goals. Sure enough, they have offered me the director of sales training here at headquarters with a package that exceeds what I had outlined for you last week.

"They would like a decision from us by the end of the week, but to be honest, I feel like a kid two days before Christmas waiting to open the biggest present under the tree. I am more than happy to wait until I get home to discuss this with you face-to -face and then respond, but honestly, would you mind talking now?" he said, finally taking a breath.

Anna smiled and quickly said, "What's there to talk about? This is a tremendous opportunity for you career-wise, and financially, it's a real winner without even factoring in what I decide to do about a new job. I am networked well enough in both long-term care and emergency medicine to land something good in a vibrant market like Kalamazoo. Grab the ring, buckaroo. Tell them it's a big yes!"

"Goddamn it, you are the absolute best thing that has ever happened to me!" shouted Tom.

"I know. Go tell them yes and get back here. We have some celebrating and planning to do," responded Anna.

No time like the present to share the good news. Anna scrolled up her boss's cell in her contacts and hit Call.

Bob picked up on the second ring and said, "Tell me your husband did not get the position at corporate."

Anna relished saying, "Well, Bob, he not only got it but he accepted on the spot, which we had agreed upon before he left. I am now ready with your sign-off to have Med List post the position on their site after I have notified my direct reports here at the facility. We have just short of ninety days to get the position filled, and I will do my best to find the very best fit for the job. What do you think?"

"I think that my day just got a whole lot worse. Do I need to come out there and speak to your people to make sure they are OK?" Bob inquired.

Shocked that he would make the drive but wanting to protect her staff from his brand of encouragement, which was usually stories about himself, she said, "I think I've got this one, but thanks. I will go ahead and get the ball rolling with filling my position if you approve."

"Yes, let's see if anyone bites, and update me weekly. Have to run." He clicked off.

Classic Struttmeir, thought Anna. No congratulations to Tom and totally absorbed in what this meant to him. While she would miss Serenity Acres horribly, she could not wait to distance herself from that self-absorbed twit.

*

Down in B wing, Dr. Penelope Lipscombe was getting acquainted with Dr. Elijah Washington at their first session of CBT. As was usually the case, it was a slow start, with her asking easy questions that he reluctantly and succinctly answered. Penelope was a little in awe of her new patient, but she quickly realized that his needs were just the same as so many others she had seen in similar situations. Helping him find new meaning to his life after losing his companion of over fifty years was absolutely possible but not at all easy. The discussion touched briefly on hobbies outside of work, and she learned that he had played the piano since childhood. She told him the reading and game room had a very fine old upright that was kept in tune mainly for Sunday services and hymn singing. He nodded, and they spoke a few more minutes before their forty-five-minute session was up. She asked him to think about what they had discussed and told him she looked forward to their meeting the following week and that he should take notes about things he would like to cover then. He nodded again, and she gently patted his shoulder as she left the room.

On her way out of the building, Penelope added her session notes to Elijah's folder at the nursing station, telling Melanie that she should think about encouraging one of the more cognitively intact and outgoing patients to visit Dr. Washington.

Melanie said, "That's a great idea, and I have the perfect candidate."

11

The Accidental Concert

Music is the divine way to tell beautiful poetic things to the heart.

—Pablo Casals

The next day, George found himself wandering down B wing, where the traffic had slowed somewhat from the initial surge to get a glimpse of the new guy in the assisted-living section. The new resident's door was open, and George stood in the doorway and saw Dr. Washington standing and looking out his window onto the courtyard and the garden.

As Dr. Lipscombe had suggested, George engaged by saying, "Wow! You are a big, dark one, aren't you?"

Elijah turned and slowly took in George, and a small smile formed on his face. "I suppose I am. Pretty sure I am still about six foot three when I don't slouch. Do you mind my asking when you had your stroke?" Elijah asked.

Somewhat surprised, George said, "Just about three years ago, and how did you know that?"

Elijah said softly, "I practiced medicine for about forty years and have seen my share of folks with what is commonly referred to as impulse control issues. Stroke is the cause of that almost exclusively in those of more advanced age."

George nodded and said, "OK. That makes sense to me. Well, I am on my way to tend to my garden, and my name is George. If you want me to give you a tour, look me up."

Elijah smiled and said, "I'm Elijah, and I might just do that at some point."

George turned and ambled off, and Elijah thought that the world could use more straight talkers like George.

*

Before making it out to his garden for the daily watering, weeding, and feeding, George literally bumped into Samantha as he was rounding a corner. George excused the mishap and then said sincerely, "You know, Samantha, something has got me a bit confused. I guess we all know that you and Melanie are wife and wife or legally married or whatever, and we think that it's great. Well, most of us, anyway. Now we hear you two are going to start a family and have a baby. Not to get too personal, but how the hell is that going to work? Are you going to find a volunteer to be the father, and if so, will that require, you know, intimacy? But I don't think that is likely given that both of you are clearly not interested in those sorts of activities with a man. The truth is, I'm not really up on all the science of reproductive medicine, and my curiosity has got my imagination working overtime, if you know what I mean. You certainly don't owe me or anyone an explanation, but quite honestly, I'm just interested."

Samantha smiled broadly and said, "George, Melanie and I are just now working through the details ourselves. Donor profiles, sperm banks, insemination techniques, and so on. All the stuff that needs to be researched and decided is somewhat overwhelming, but we are very excited. How about when we get a little further down the line, we sit down and describe everything to you and anyone else who is interested? Do you think that any other residents would be curious as well?"

George shared, "Oh, I know they are. It would be a packed house. To tell you the truth, you had me at sperm banks. I bet you Cookie would cater the whole thing just to sit in herself!"

Samantha beamed and said, "Well, I bet it will be the first fertility seminar given at a senior living facility. Can't wait."

*

Two mornings later, at around 7:30 in the reading and game room, the alluring sound of George Gershwin's *Rhapsody in Blue* began floating out of the door and down both wings of Serenity Acres. The piece started slow and soft and began building as it progressed in both pace and intensity. Elijah Washington knew it by heart, all sixteen minutes of the piano solo version. The first to peek in and then take seats were the Vera Bradley Bridge Mafia. They politely sat and listened, mesmerized by the music and skill. Pretty soon, George, June, and a host of other walker-pushing enthusiasts had found seats to enjoy the unexpected impromptu concert. The audience certainly recognized Gershwin's 1924 masterpiece that is generally acknowledged as one of if not *the* greatest pieces of American music composed in the twentieth century. They did not know that it was composed in less than forty-five days and performed the first time by Gershwin with Paul Whiteman and his Palais Royal Band at Aeolian Hall in NYC to an audience that included

Rachmaninov, Leopold Stokowski, and Fritz Kreisler. Elijah knew that, and it was one of many reasons he loved the piece. The audience only knew that the music flowed from the piano played by the tall black man and gave them a warm and wonderful feeling. When the crescendo at the end of the piece built and finally stopped, Elijah sat for about a full minute and enjoyed Gershwin's gift once more. He finally turned and was shocked to find about twenty-five residents sitting wide-eyed and in awe of what they had just heard. He scanned the crowd side to side, nodded, and then headed for the door, only to be stopped by George, who introduced him as his friend Dr. Elijah Washington. Then, with plenty of volume for all to hear, he asked Elijah if he had gotten permission from United Airlines to play their theme song.

"No, the composer and I have been friends for a long, long time," he said pensively and walked out.

12

Observation Time

Most of the successful people I have known are the ones who do more listening than talking.

—Bernard Baruch

Although Elijah had only left his room once in the first two weeks since his arrival at Serenity Acres, that didn't mean he hadn't picked up on things. He was, above all other things, a skilled listener, something he had learned from his father. Never had he heard his father interrupt someone or finish a sentence for them. Asa was a man who truly wanted to understand what someone thought or felt. From his room, Dr. Washington had taken in multiple days of activity in the courtyard garden through his window. He had witnessed multiple games of bridge, always played by the same four attractive ladies seated in the same positions each time. Residents in wheelchairs, pushing walkers, leaning on canes, and ambling slowly all took in the spectacular array of horticulture tended lovingly by his friend with the impulse control issue. His guess was that it was more than a hobby for George. While he missed the audio portion in most of these observations, he got a good sense of the mood, ebbs, and flows of the place. It was like life elsewhere, but at a much slower pace set by its bent and gray inhabitants. He could sense a quiet contentment and happiness and was impressed by the independence of even the more infirm residents. *Good things are taking place here,* he thought.

By confining himself to his room, he had not been able to determine the source of the mournful requests for help that came from the direction of A wing, not far from his own door. He surprised the LPN who removed his food trays each day by not only talking but asking about the resident making the requests. The LPN said it was Screaming Edgar, that he was pretty far down the dementia road, and that it had been occurring almost daily and sometimes hourly. Elijah thanked her and reached into his bedside table, where Dr. Lipscombe had left a pen and pad for him to make notes about his own situation. He grabbed his robe and walked down the hall to the beginning of B wing by the central nursing station and only had to listen for a few minutes before Edgar made his request. Dr. Washington then asked for a chair, which the nurse provided, and set it up across the hall from Edgar's door and began his observation. Dr. Washington noted each time that the plea for help came and what was happening in the hallway. After two hours, he had all the data he needed, and he scooted the chair back to the nursing station, said thanks, and strolled back down to his room.

That afternoon, Dr. Lipscombe came for their scheduled CBT session and began with the usual questions about his time since they'd last met, how he was feeling, and if he had made any notes that might assist in their discussion.

He replied, "I did make some notes that involve environmental observations of another resident who seems distressed. At the intersection of the two wings, there is a resident whose first name is Edgar. He frequently makes requests for help, which I can hear from my room. I spent two hours close to his door this morning to determine what the cause of his distress is and whether it is possible to mitigate his discomfort in any way. This crude chart represents each incidence Edgar asked for help and what was occurring outside his door at the time. As you can see, Doctor, there was foot traffic sometimes accompanied by conversation just before Edgar made each request. My guess would be that even in his diminished state, he is simply asking for someone to sit with him. Knowing that staff can't give that kind of time, it would seem logical to consider moving Edgar to a less-trafficked portion of the hallway. Perhaps one of the rooms on the end of A wing could be made available. I believe he would be less agitated and everyone else less annoyed by his continual petitions."

Stunned momentarily, Penelope finally said, "That is the most you have talked since you have arrived, and it had nothing to do with your own situation. I find the insight valuable and the fact that you took the time to do what you did most admirable. I also understand that you gave quite a performance on the piano the other morning. Were you going to mention that to me?"

"Nice to see the staff here paying attention and adding it to a patient chart. Yes, a few residents came in while I was absorbed in a rather long piece and seemed to enjoy my efforts. If you don't ask too many more questions, I might even venture down there again and play something else. You know the rumor is that music is quite therapeutic," Elijah quipped.

"You are a deep man, Dr. Washington. I will look forward to seeing you next time," Penelope said.

"Deep, huh? I guess life can do that to you. Have a good day, Doctor," said Elijah warmly.

As Dr. Lipscombe walked away, she thought Elijah's depression might just be conquered by his involvement with the other residents.

Dr. Washington decided to shower and dress if for no other reason than because he still was someone who liked to look presentable. He looked out his window into the courtyard garden, and there was George with a wide-brimmed hat working on a large green bush with beautiful white snowball-shaped flowers. Elijah decided it was nice out, and if he was just going to sit in his room otherwise, why not get some fresh air and go out and watch George? He walked from his room, hoping to escape notice, which was unlikely for a tall black man to do anywhere in Hidden Falls.

Quietly approaching George, who was busy pruning the same bush, Dr. Washington asked, "Is the offer for a tour of your garden still good?"

"Anytime for you is good, Doc. Let me finish with the big fella here, and we can take in the grounds. This is one of my hardy broad-leaf hydrangeas. The blooms are currently all white, but I am attempting to alter the soil pH to get some blue and pink. I like a mix of color. Makes the world so much more interesting. Don't you think?" George said without breaking a smile.

George got up slowly from working on the hydrangea, brushed off his kneeling pads, and motioned for Dr. Washington to follow. They veered right and were quickly on a crushed vermiculite path that wound through a rose garden containing what appeared to be at least fifty different rosebushes. The colors were stunning, and Elijah just stopped and turned slowly, taking them in. All the bushes were labeled (Cherry Parfait, Teasing Georgia, Rainbow Knockout, and on and on), and the colors were mixed to create an almost artist-palette effect with the path as the frame of the picture.

The doctor finally finished his visual feast and looked back at George and asked, "So what did you do before you got here, my friend?"

"Would it surprise you if I told you I was a landscaper?" George replied.

"Not one bit, and I might add the qualifier a damn good one," declared Elijah.

"You know, Doc, I discovered that continuing to do the things I love and am fairly good at did two things for me. First, it gave me a reason and purpose, which we all need. Second, it seemed to lift all my fellow detainees here at Serenity Acres, and I realized that is pretty gratifying. Especially when the other contribution that I make is to blurt things out that aren't always appreciated."

"George, you are a generous man, and your willingness to share things of a personal nature carry as much value as your incredible horticultural talents," Elijah said sincerely.

"You know, Doc, I think we could become pretty close friends," said George quietly.

"Indeed, indeed," confirmed Elijah.

13

In Case You Forgot, It's All About Me

We can't all be stars because someone has to sit on the curb and clap as I go by.

—Sebastian Horsley

Bob Struttmeir and his peers sat around the long conference room table in the boardroom of Silver Age Industries in King of Prussia, Pennsylvania, on the outskirts of Philadelphia. They were there for their biannual meeting with their boss, Kirsten Stanley, the chief operating officer of Silver Age, and were reviewing their financial performance, quality scores, and any important personnel issues. Bob sat midtable and listened semi-attentively as his colleagues covered their regions. When it was his time in the bucket, he enthusiastically talked about his financials, which currently ranked second among the regions, and his quality scores, which ranked third, thus placing him on a combined basis as the number-one region in country. Then, thanks to his ungrateful administrator in Hidden Falls, he had to report that he was losing her due to a promotion her husband received to Stryker headquarters in Kalamazoo. Everyone knew that Serenity Acres was his top-performing facility in both measures and took quiet joy in his loss. Bob was not anyone's favorite regional VP, and in fact, he was generally regarded as a perfect asshole by each of his colleagues. To confirm that, Rory Johnson from the mid-Atlantic region asked if that was the facility that had taken six months to fill the administrator roll a few years earlier. Bob turned red and answered that he didn't remember the amount of time it took, but he had constructed a great replacement strategy with corporate HR, and he expected no problems with the opening. Unbeknownst to Bob, Kirsten had been informed by HR that they were working closely with Anna Halstead, who had formulated a good recruiting plan and was beginning to collect candidates surfaced by the same online health-care recruiting firm that had delivered her.

Kirsten smiled inwardly and then offered, "That's smart, Bob. It would be good for you to provide me with weekly updates on the progress in filling Anna's position. That is a strategic loss for Silver Age."

"Absolutely, Kirsten. We will find the right person quickly and not lose any performance from Serenity Acres on the financial or quality sides," said Bob. He was already planning a call to Anna back in Hidden

Falls at their first break, and she'd better damn well have a positive update.

*

Anna had a good start to the morning, when her cell rang and she saw that it was Bob. Philosophically, she figured that when one was as blessed as she was with a super family, true friends, and a great work environment, the universe would always remind you that there were also dark forces at play everywhere. Bob was her dark force. So with her usual bright and cheerful tone, she answered her cell, knowing that alone would piss the Struttmeister off.

"Hey, boss! How is the weather out there in King of Prussia?" she chirped.

Feeling the veins in his forehead pulse from his bench in the courtyard of the headquarters building, he stated, "Not the time to talk weather, Ms. Halstead. I need a quick and thorough update on our progress with recruiting your replacement."

"Sure enough, Mr. Struttmeir. Would you like it verbally right now, or should I e-mail you a bulleted outline of progress to date?"

"Get it to me in an e-mail in the next ten minutes," barked the prick, and he clicked off.

This once again verified for Anna that not having him as a boss any longer would be the rough equivalent of having a boil removed from one's ass, allowing for comfortable sitting. After a long, cleansing breath, she composed a succinct overview of her interface with Med List, the job posting, the three responses to date, and finally her phone screening schedule with each of the applicants. Within eight minutes, she had sent the e-mail to Bob. Exactly two minutes later, her phone chimed again, with her boss on the other end.

With no greeting, he said, "I want those phone screens done today and any viable candidates passed on to corporate HR ASAP. When I agreed to having you run the front end of this search, I thought you would have had greater sense of urgency. Do you understand?"

Barely containing her urge to crawl through the line and strangle the asshole, Anna said, "Please accept my apologies. I have been busy running your number-one facility with a staff of twenty plus and nearly one hundred residents. Your request will be honored, and the results forwarded as you indicated. Will there be anything else?"

Slightly shaken and not as aggressive, Struttmeir started to respond when he realized she had left the call.

Anna sat silently for a few minutes, thinking about the professional way to pass on her opinions of her boss upon her exit. She would figure that out when the time came, but at that moment, she needed to get back to what she loved and center herself in something positive. She left her office and told Bonnie she was off on a walkabout, a term she borrowed from one of her favorite Australian movies starring Nicole Kidman and Hugh Jackman. When she got to the intersection of the two wings, she walked down to the end of A wing and stuck her head into Edgar Vornoy's room. He was resting easily with his eyes open, and he stirred slightly as she approached the bed. She pulled up the side chair and gently took his hand in hers as she sat down. Moving him down to this room had been an obvious solution to his agitation caused by the foot traffic and noise in the middle of the facility. As Edgar rested easily for the ten minutes or so, she thought about how this solution had come about. Dr. Lipscombe had been informed of the cause of his discomfort by Dr. Washington, who had taken the time to observe and document even though he himself was a resident. There was something there that needed to be explored.

14

A Whole New World

You know children are growing up when they stop asking you where they came from and refuse to tell you where they are going.

—P. J. O'Rourke

As promised by Samantha, the "Fertility Symposium" was scheduled, and the day had arrived for the unique presentation to anyone from Serenity Acres who was interested. It was being held in the reading and game room, and flyers were posted with a cute picture of Melanie and Samantha holding hands, the time of the presentation, and a promise of refreshments. Just like George had predicted, the turnout was robust, with about thirty-five fascinated residents there early and already eyeing the range of fresh-baked pies provided by their very own Cookie Klemposki. Someone clinked a glass with a fork, and Melanie and Samantha took their places behind the eight-foot table flanked by two interesting posters.

Anna started with an introduction. "Welcome to all. I am excited to introduce two special people we all know and love—Melanie Grogan Smith and Samantha Smith Grogan. Many of you have expressed interest in the journey they are just now undertaking, which is to start a family. At the same time, many have a lot of questions about the process and how it all comes together. These two have graciously offered to give a brief but informative presentation on the subject and take any questions you may have. So I will turn it over to the two best nursing managers any administrator could ever hope to have—Samantha and Melanie!"

Samantha started by explaining the two posters flanking the table. The one on their right dealt with the process, source, and selection of a donor and had a picture of a structure labeled *Sperm Bank*, which had George on the edge of his seat. The poster on the left had an interesting diagram of a medical apparatus attached to a uterus, or lady part, if you preferred. They both took time to describe their trip to Madison and the fertility clinic. Melanie gave a great description of the counselor who took them through the selection criteria and database that listed the 1,500-plus donors their inventory represented. Samantha shared that their preferred profile included graduate-degreed, taller-than-average, Caucasian individuals who were mathematically and musically inclined.

A brave soul seated in the front row and sitting next to Dr. Washington asked why they had specified Caucasian. Samantha calmly answered that they both agreed that having two mothers was enough for the average child to answer to in central Wisconsin without being mixed race as well. Elijah smiled and nodded his understanding and agreement.

Inevitably, George's hand went up, and the whole room braced for what would undoubtedly be a showstopper of a question. George started with a quick story about a buddy of his who delivered a sperm sample in a Miracle Whip jar, following a vasectomy, to his doctor's office for fertility lab work. He wondered how and where the bank collected their specimens. Without missing a beat, Melanie said that donors were required to deliver and produce on-site so as to assure the authenticity and integrity of the specimen. The whole room seemed both satisfied and relieved to move on to the next section. Melanie then stood and walked over to the chart representing the sperm delivery mechanism and its route to deep in the uterus. As she described the placement of the sperm into a syringe with media and the insertion of the very slender catheter up the vagina, through the cervix, and all the way to the uterus, three members of the Vera Bradley Bridge Mafia began frantically fanning themselves while Suzanne, along with Dr. Washington, watched them with amusement.

Following the description of that process, June Wilhelm asked perhaps the best question of the session, which was how the two of them were deciding who would undergo the intrauterine insemination procedure and what criteria they used for that decision. Melanie acknowledged the quality of what June had asked and explained that Samantha's lower cervix was longer and as such removed more risk of a premature delivery, and therefore, Samantha would carry the baby. The tempo of the fanning once again approached hummingbird wing speed as the meeting mercifully rolled to a conclusion. Everyone broke ranks and headed for Cookie's pie table, where generous wedges were being served with whipped cream on top. Suzanne made her way across the room to where George and Elijah were enjoying the fruits of Cookie's labor and introduced herself to Dr. Washington. She asked Elijah if he was surprised that a senior center would have a fertility discussion. He calmly said that nothing happening there surprised him, and while the subject of procreation was probably beyond utility for most of those assembled, the fascination and curiosity were certainly not. He then smiled and left.

*

Later that afternoon, Anna was at her desk thinking about the remarkable session that she had witnessed that morning in the reading and game room. Most if not all of the attendees were born close to the end of World War II. There early worlds were filled with the new marvel of television, the heating up of the Cold War, the explosion on the scene of rock and roll, the cultural revolution, and a host of other changes. Maybe that's why they were so interested but not confused or upset by two women marrying each other, starting a family by shopping for the right gene pool of the father, and finally undergoing a pretty complex process of fertilization. She shook her head and thought just for a moment that this reaction was made possible by the environment she had helped create, and she was proud. Scanning her e-mail, she noticed a new request from Kirsten Stanley to give her a call when she had a moment. Anna closed her door and dialed on her cell and was surprised when Kirsten's administrative assistant put her immediately through to the COO.

"Thanks for getting back to me so quickly, Anna. While I am truly sorry you will be leaving, it sounds like a great opportunity for Tom, and

I am genuinely happy for your family. How are things going there at the facility?"

Anna shared an overview of the fertility symposium they'd held that morning, and Kirsten was both humored and impressed but not surprised. She had grown to expect that type of outside-the-box thinking from Anna and her team, to which she attributed Serenity Acres' unique environment and success. Before they ended the call, Kirsten requested to be kept in the loop with the progress they were making on finding a replacement by being BCC'd on Anna's e-mail updates to Bob. The request didn't surprise Anna, because she knew that Kirsten's bullshit sensors were acute and was confident that they were on high alert every time Struttmeir opened his mouth.

15

Take Me Out to the Ball Game

I'd give my right arm to be ambidextrous.

—Yogi Berra

Elijah sat quietly in Edgar Vornoy's room, leafing through a scrapbook from his bedside table. He had visited Edgar every day for a few minutes, sometimes offering a comment or question to the dazed and bedridden skeletal figure under the sheet and thin blanket. Dr. Washington had no expectation of a response but believed that Edgar could still sense human presence and interaction, which might somehow bring comfort. Today he was concentrating on the Edgar's scrapbook with genuine interest and admiration. Elijah was a baseball fan—the Chicago Cubs, to be exact. The scrapbook covered Edgar's career with the Wausau Lumberjacks minor-league team (now known as the Wausau Woodchucks) from 1955 through 1965 as one of their starting pitchers. Articles were included from the *Wausau Daily Herald* that highlighted particularly good outings by Edgar, and some had his picture, showing him as a handsome and smiling young man. One article from the 1970s was an interview with Edgar that talked about playing briefly with Vada Pinson—who, for one season at the age of seventeen, played with the Lumberjacks before moving up to the bigs. His comments were insightful and generous and made Elijah wish that he could talk with the still figure who breathed steadily in the bed next to him.

On his way back to his room, Elijah bumped into Anna, who was making her midmorning rounds, and she mentioned that it was nice he was spending time with Edgar. Dr. Washington smiled slightly and mentioned the scrapbook and a bit about Edgar's baseball career. Then he surprised Anna by asking if it would be possible for him to talk with Edgar's next of kin to learn more about his past and his baseball experiences. Anna thought only briefly and then said that she would contact his daughter, who lived in Wausau, and ask if it was OK for Elijah to call her. Elijah nodded, excused himself, and walked back to his room.

Anna made sure to enter Dr. Washington's visits to Edgar in Elijah's patient chart, as this activity would be of real interest to Penelope Lipscombe. Just so she wouldn't forget, she pulled Edgar's file and gave his daughter a call as soon as she got back to her office. She caught her on her cell during her lunch break, and she assured her that her father's condition had not changed and she was calling with a request from another patient who had grown interested in Edgar's baseball days. Anna briefly described Dr. Washington and told Edgar's daughter how he had suggested the room change to keep her father calm and was now spending some time each day looking at his minor-league scrapbook and talking to Edgar about his exploits. His daughter was genuinely touched and offered to send another box of memorabilia from the Lumberjack days that afternoon and gave her unconditional approval to Elijah to call her anytime, because she wanted to thank him personally.

*

At 10:00 the next morning, FedEx delivered a banker's box to the office of Serenity Acres, addressed to Dr. Elijah Washington. Bonnie asked if she could walk it down to Elijah's room, and Anna smiled and said of course. Bonnie hustled out the door and within two minutes was standing in Dr. Washington's doorway. Elijah looked up from his chair by the window and waved her in. Bonnie explained that the box was from Edgar's daughter, Daphne Pritchard, and that it was addressed to him personally. Then she left him to it.

Elijah stood over the box and used his house key to split the tape of the middle seam. Under the bubble wrap was a vintage Rawlings fielder's glove with *Vornoy* written along the left outside finger in a neat hand. There were multiple Lumberjack game programs, and at the bottom of the box was a small-framed picture with a young Edgar in his Lumberjack uniform, posing with a slender black player in an Anchorage Earthquake uniform. On the back, it read, "1966," and in longhand, "Posing with my new friend Satchel Paige after our exhibition game in Toronto."

"Holy shit!" whispered Elijah.

Taped to the front of picture was a sticky note with Daphne's number and a request to call upon receipt. Elijah sat back down in his chair with the picture in his lap and dialed. Daphne picked up after three rings, and Elijah introduced himself.

There was a pause, and then Daphne started, "I was so surprised when Anna called and explained about your involvement with Dad. Candidly, I have felt terrible about him being there and me a few hours away and unable to see him very often. He was and is the greatest father anyone could ever hope for. He taught me everything I know about working hard and being self-reliant. After baseball, he worked in the insurance business here in Wausau for almost forty years until retiring. He and my mom were both tremendous people. All our friends were always at our house, and I'm pretty sure it was because they trusted my parents, unlike most other adults.

"Anyway, after my mom passed, Dad lived alone for a few years, and then he started to have trouble caring for himself—eating, bathing, remembering to pay the bills, and finally even staying in touch with friends and those close to him. So my brother and I made the hard decision just about three years ago, and it has torn me up every time I wonder how he is doing. To know that he has a friend is just so wonderful. I'm sorry I am blubbering on and being so emotional. It's just hard."

Elijah said gently, "Daphne, let me share something with you. I'm here because I am lucky enough to have a daughter that loves me as much as you love your dad. I lost my wife down in Chicago and spiraled into a dark place about two months ago. My daughter is the medical director of one of the busiest ERs in Chicago and knew she didn't have the time to nurse me back to some semblance of normalcy, so she sent me up here to Anna and Serenity Acres, where luckily I got to know your dad. We actually have a lot in common: great daughters, a love of baseball, and a hole in our lives left by the passing of beautiful wives. When you are here, I look forward to sharing more. In the meantime, I will update you from time to time about what Edgar and I are discussing. Please understand the conversation is really me asking him questions and then speculating myself on what the answer might be. I am of the belief that the human consciousness is often awake and functioning even when there are no outward indications. He and I will have a conversation every day. You also need to know that he is helping me by being here in his own way. I really mean that. Does that make sense to you?"

"Yes, Dr. Washington, and you don't know how much I appreciate your companionship to my father. We will talk soon, and in the meantime, may God bless you and keep you, sir," said Daphne, her voice trembling.

"Oh, he already has, child. He already has," replied Elijah, who meant what he said.

After the call, Elijah texted Angela. He then thumbed out the following:

Dear Dr. Washington,

When you get time, would you drop by the house and pick up the picture of your grandfather and the tall, well-dressed black man in the Pullman dining car, on top of my dresser in my closet? I am eating and doing a bit better. Thanks for sending me to the "Russian front." Feels like med school ... the only brother within miles.

Love,

Dad

*

Down the hallway, Anna was engaged with the Med List account rep on strategies to surface more candidates for her upcoming vacancy. Of the three that had surfaced so far, she had only sent one on to corporate for screening, and that had gone nowhere when the issue of salary was broached. She had kept Kirsten in the loop as she had suggested regarding her communications with Struttmeir and was dreading her next conversation with him if someone didn't turn up soon. Then, just to get her mind off that subject, she called Dr. MacDonald to find out when he was coming by the facility again. She had an idea that might just benefit all concerned.

16

New Friends and New Ideas

Be willing to be a beginner every single morning.

—Meister Eckhart

Dr. Ian MacDonald hadn't been out to see either of his two patients and interface with staff at Serenity Acres for at least a week, and he desperately needed a break, so he called Anna and asked what was for lunch. As soon as he got to the facility, he went to the central nursing station and asked for his two new patients' charts and the other four the practice was on record as caring for. Samantha greeted him warmly and told him he was welcome to spread those out in the consultation room behind the chest-level work counter and the staff computer stations. He thanked her and gathered them up and walked into the surprisingly spacious and well-equipped room. He pulled over a stool to the exam table and leafed through his two new patients' files first and then quickly checked the names and general status of his other four charges. Anna poked her head in, saying that the rumors were true that a handsome young man impersonating a doctor had been sighted in her building. He laughed and asked if she would buy him lunch down at the dining hall after he checked on his various charges. She said, "Sure," and she was going to invite someone else to join them that she wanted Ian to meet. Thirty minutes later, he messaged her and said he was done with rounds and needed to eat.

Anna responded that she would see him down there. On the way to the dining room, she stopped by Dr. Washington's room and told him that she wanted him to meet and have lunch with a friend of hers. He started to object, but she convinced him into tagging along.

They met Dr. MacDonald at the dining room entrance, where Anna made the introductions. She led them over to a nice round table by the french doors, and they settled in. Cookie hustled over to inform them she had outdone herself with the Southern fried chicken, mashed potatoes, and corn and that they should all try it. No one objected, and she hustled off. Dr. MacDonald asked if it would be OK to talk just a little business before the food came. Neither Anna nor Elijah objected, so he quickly started.

"Really pleased with our two newbies and how they have settled in here. Melanie, Samantha, and Penelope were right about the CBT approach with lower antidepressant doses for both on the front end. I would like their opinion of tapering off the Lexapro over the next couple of weeks. If they concur, I will write a new pharmacy order. I quickly introduced myself to the other four patients that the practice manages. They were all polite enough to not act too disappointed at losing my predecessor as their physician. I was thinking that over the next month, I would come back and do a quick exam and workup on each. Would you mind if I used the consult room, which, by the way, is nicer than my office?"

Anna laughed and said he was welcome anytime to use the consult room.

Dr. MacDonald looked across the table to Dr. Washington and said, "Doctor, I have to admit I am kind of starstruck sitting here getting ready to have lunch with one of the legends of Chicago medicine. If you don't mind my asking, how are you getting along?"

"Well, Ian, you are both entitled and qualified to tender that question. Last time I checked, that is more or less what doctors do. Anna, the staff, and the residents have been nothing but kind to this old man. Cookie has managed to put some weight back on these bones, which has afforded a bit more energy, and I have slowly become less of a recluse. So my prognosis appears to be improving, but I'm not yet out of the woods."

"You know, I'm not sure if you would be interested, but I would love to have you come and see my practice. I am new at it, and I discovered that just about 65 percent of what you have to figure out isn't covered at med school or a residency. The coffee is bad, and the decor is straight out of *The Andy Griffith Show*, but I still think there is potential."

"Well, getting out a bit is beginning to have some appeal, and the rumor here at the home is that you have a brand-new Audi A8 Quattro, which wouldn't be bad to experience," quipped Elijah.

"Great! I'll call you in a few days and set it up. Now here comes Cookie with a tray of goodness that we need to attend to," said Dr. MacDonald.

*

Later that afternoon, a FedEx package arrived for Elijah, which he took back to his room to open. It was from Angela, and he assumed it was the picture he had requested. He discovered that indeed she had sent the picture of Asa Washington and Satchel Paige, dated 1948. Underneath the picture was his leather journal, which he had quit making entries in specifically on March 14 of this year when his beautiful wife, Sandra, had died. The note attached to the front in Angela's distinctive hand read:

> Good to know that you are starting to interact with others and gaining back some much-needed weight. Not surprised that you are carefully observing others and making helpful suggestions on how to improve their circumstances—that is what you do. Might be good to get back to observing yourself and making some notes in your journal. Rest assured, I DID NOT even open the cover. My opinion is that your suggestions to yourself might be just as helpful as your ideas for others.
>
> Love you,
> Angela

Elijah thought that he and Sandra had raised a very insightful and nice human being.

17

We All Are Connected in Some Way

Six Degrees of Separation is the idea that all living things and everything else in the world are six or fewer steps away from each other so that a chain of a "friend of a friend" statements can be made to connect any two people in maximum of six steps.

—Frigyes Karinthy, Hungary, 1929

Dr. Washington was excited to take his picture to Edgar's room; he wanted to show it to him and share the story. He entered Edgar's room and went to the bedside table, where he had placed the picture of Edgar and Satchel Paige in Toronto in 1966. He put that with his picture of Asa Washington and Satchel Paige from 1948 in a Pullman dining car on a trip from Chicago to Cleveland. Sitting beside the bed, he shook his head with wonder and began talking to Edgar.

"You know, Edgar, I think it is just incredible that here you and I are in 2018 becoming friends, and we are both connected to one of the great baseball players of all time. Satchel traveled on my dad's train to

Cleveland to join the Cleveland Indians, thanks to Jackie Robinson and Branch Rickey. Satchel Paige played professional baseball from 1923, when he was released from reform school in Alabama, to 1966, when he was fifty-nine years old and pitched for the Kansas City Athletics. He loved the game whether he was playing for peanuts in the Negro Leagues or finally pitching in the World Series for the Indians in 1948, which they won in six games. His career is not just amazing due to its length but also for his love of the game and his attitude in the face of adversity. He represented the best of what baseball can be and did it with panache and grace.

"Now here you and I sit, decades past his career, sharing a tangible connection to the man. I'm not sure what this signifies. Maybe it's just that if you live long enough, you will encounter people who share something from your past that meant something. My dad had a long career with the Pullman Company and worked his way up in the Brotherhood of Sleeping Car Porters to a position of some importance. But I think the single greatest moment of his career was his meeting and brief friendship with Satchel Paige. They both shared a past that few of us can even understand today. I have had my troubles recently due to the passing of my wife a few months back. Meeting you and discovering this thing we have in common is helping me to get things back in perspective. I just want you to know that, my friend."

For just a second, Elijah thought Edgar was smiling. Dr. Washington moved the two pictures from the over bed table and put them up on Edgar's dresser. He patted Edgar's hand and made his way out to the hallway, where he discovered Suzanne Holmby, who seemed a bit embarrassed.

"Oh, hello, Dr. Washington. I'm afraid you caught me eavesdropping just a bit. I was strolling the corridors and heard you speaking with Edgar and got caught up in the conversation. Please accept my apology," Suzanne offered.

Elijah thought briefly and then said, "Not to worry, Suzanne. Edgar and I were just sharing some common history. We are not planning the armed overthrow of the facility until next week sometime."

Relieved that she had been absolved of any serious busybody infraction, she replied, "It has always fascinated me how we are all connected in such surprising ways. Do you think Edgar understands anything you are offering?"

"You know, honestly, I'm not sure. The mind is an incredible thing and will constantly confound those who profess to understand how and why it functions. In any event, it gives me an opportunity to talk about things that interest me, and it just maybe affords some company to my friend Edgar."

"Well, that's awfully kind of you, Dr. Washington, and if you ever feel like covering another topic with someone who might ask a question or venture an opinion, I'm available," said Suzanne.

"That's the best offer I've had in a while, Suzanne, and please call me Elijah. I left my white coat back in Chicago."

*

Feeling better than he had in some time, Elijah looked at his watch and decided he might drop by the reading and game room and play a little. When he got there, he noticed a few fellow residents reading quietly and started to leave.

June Wilhelm was one of them, and she looked up and said, "Come back here, Dr. Washington. It's a common room, which essentially means it is designed to be used by all of us. If you were coming in to play something, I personally would love to hear some good jazz."

"So you are a jazz fan, young lady? What would you like to hear?"

"You had me at *young lady*, Dr. Washington. You choose. I have a feeling you know the subject a bit better than I do." June smiled.

Elijah approached the piano, going over his favorite jazz pieces in his head. The third song he thought about seemed to fit the mood. "Take Five" written in 5/4 time by Paul Desmond, who played alto sax in Dave Brubeck's jazz ensemble, was the most famous cut off Brubeck's iconic album *Time Out*. He launched into the herky-jerky rhythm of the song that was performed on *The Ed Sullivan Show* in 1962 after spending twelve weeks in the Top 100 in 1961, an unusual accomplishment for a jazz piece.

Elijah was quickly into the light and fluid portion that reminded June of her youth and had others who were coming in tapping a toe or snapping a finger and remembering their youth as well. The adaptation to piano only is tricky, as the melody is really written for alto sax, but that's why Elijah loved the challenge of re-creating it on piano only.

When he finished, there was polite applause, and June said, "Delightful, Dr. Washington. Simply delightful."

He stood and said, "June, call me Elijah. Sounds much more appropriate for a jazz musician, don't you think?" He winked and left for the dining room.

18

Different Generations, Same Goals

Teach them the quiet words of kindness, to live beyond themselves. Urge them toward excellence, drive them toward gentleness, pull them deep into yourself, pull them upward toward manhood, but softly like an angel arranging clouds. Let your spirit move through them softly.

—Pat Conroy, *The Prince of Tides*

Elijah was looking forward to his half day visiting Ian MacDonald's practice. Truth be told, his own experience was a big-city practice that involved much time spent in major hospitals and the various organizational demands that grew out of those environments. He secretly had always relished the idea of the family practice doctor in a smaller town, but he was enough of a realist to know that his vision certainly lacked any real knowledge of the challenges that surely existed there as well. When Ian picked him up, Elijah was indeed impressed with the interior finishes and electronics in the Audi. Elijah asked about Ian's family and was informed he had a newly born son and a stay-at-home wife, who was adjusting to life in small-town Wisconsin.

Ian took a small detour past his new house on the way to his practice, just off the town square. Ian was proud of the vintage Sears kit home they had purchased, which was built in 1920 and had the classic craftsman bungalow design elements. Elijah shared that his home in Oak Park was one of the forerunners of that whole design movement and was built in 1913, intentionally neglecting to mention it was in fact an original Frank Lloyd Wright–designed and -built landmark. The neighborhood was tree lined and welcoming, and Ian stated that Anna and her husband had a similar home about two blocks over.

In another five minutes, they pulled into the parking lot of a single-story office complex that primarily housed legal offices and Dr. MacDonald's newly acquired family practice. Ian introduced Dr. Washington to two nurses, who were the entirety of his office staff. The older of the two appeared to work the front desk, which consisted of answering the phone, making appointments, checking people in, and organizing and completing all the paperwork. The second was younger and was involved with hands-on evaluations and care of patients in advance of seeing the doctor.

Ian left Elijah with Beverly, the nurse / receptionist / office manager, and headed back to start through his morning appointments.

Dr. Washington took up a spot behind the counter and simply observed the flow of patients into the waiting area, their interface with Beverly, her general organization of the practice's paperwork, and the tone of the interactions. After about forty-five minutes, there was a break in the action, and Elijah engaged Beverly.

"So, Beverly, you sure have a lot of different things to juggle. How long have you been doing this, if you don't mind my asking?" queried Dr. Washington.

With a sigh and a shake of the head, Beverly answered, "I came to work for Dr. Houston, the gentleman Dr. MacDonald bought out, about twenty-five years ago. I have seen quite a few changes, most of which haven't been for the better. More paperwork, more unnecessary rules, fewer payments, more demanding patients, and longer hours. Health care, like everything else in this country, has been ruined by the government."

My, my, thought Elijah, *what a ray of sunshine we have here as the face of Dr. MacDonald's practice.* Dr. Washington then asked about the EHR system they used in the practice, and Beverly went into a lengthy diatribe on MedConnection. Apparently, Dr. Houston had the system installed three years earlier, and according to Beverly, it was hard to use and didn't really support the key areas of billing, patient records, and coding in the way they advertised. Dr. Washington then made the mistake of asking about how busy the practice was, and a fairly large vein in Beverly's forehead began to pulse as she described the frenetic pace at which patients were scheduled in the average day. It was based on twenty-minute time slots starting at 8:00 a.m. and ending at 5:30 p.m., which netted twenty-five office visits after reducing thirty minutes each for lunch and paperwork cleanup at the end of the day. While it sounded pretty reasonable to Dr. Washington, according to Beverly, it was bordering on sweatshop conditions right here in Hidden Valley, Wisconsin. Just when Elijah was thinking about how long it would take him to walk the three or four miles between the office and Serenity Acres, Dr. MacDonald showed up and asked if he were hungry. Dr. Washington exaggerated by saying he was famished, and Ian led him out of the office and around the corner to a little café on the square.

After they were seated, Dr. MacDonald opened by asking Elijah what his initial observations were from that morning. Dr. Washington started by asking Ian his impressions of his patient-care nurse, who worked directly with patients alongside him.

"Well, she is young but gaining confidence, and patients really seem to connect with her. I also like the way she is constantly asking questions about diagnoses and treatment options. With only a short window to develop an opinion, I would say she is growing nicely and is someone I would hate to lose," answered Dr. MacDonald.

There was brief silence as Dr. Washington measured his words carefully. "Tell me, Ian, what is your opinion of Beverly?" asked Elijah.

"Well, in all candor, not quite as rosy as the picture I just gave you of Cindy. Interestingly enough, I shared with my wife last night that I wasn't sure about Beverly on multiple fronts. Our billing is pretty screwed up, causing a bit of a cash flow issue. We seem to have way too much paper, given the EHR system. Lastly and most concerning is just the general tone I seem to get when she is speaking with patients, Cindy, and even me sometimes. What is your take on that, if I may ask?"

"None of what you just shared surprises me, Ian. It appears to me that Beverly may have stayed too long at the dance, if you know what I mean. I'm not sure how long she has hated her job, but the fact that she does is indisputable and pretty much oozes out of her. Seems to me that you, Cindy, and most importantly your patients deserve better."

"You know, your straightforward opinion is valued and appreciated. I had a feeling that this was probably where I would find myself. The issue is that I haven't really managed people before, and I'm not sure how to execute a termination in a way that is fair but also mitigates my risk. With your experience, what would you recommend?"

"Three things come to mind. It looks like you have at least a half dozen legal firms in your own building. Find out which one has experience with labor law and make an appointment. Secondly, talk to Anna and share your situation with her confidentially. She has been running a much larger enterprise for five years, and I would bet she has faced what you are facing multiple times. Seek her counsel. Lastly, check with the local community college or business school about sharp recent grads from their bookkeeping or accounting programs. The position requires someone with familiarity with software programs and processes, and that specialty would certainly have those types. If you find a good candidate, offer them more than you think you need to, and share what you would like to see the practice grow into. Those are things that I would consider."

Dr. MacDonald nodded his head, smiled, and said, "Why aren't you thinking about getting back on the horse? You probably have forgotten more about medicine, management, and life in general than the average guy will ever know. As a matter of fact, I'm not sure I can even afford this advice, given your CV."

"Thanks for the compliment, Doctor, and all the advice will cost you is your friendship and the Cobb salad you are about ready to buy me. Sound like a deal?"

19

The World's Greatest Treasures Are Found All Around Us

The earth has its music for those that will listen.

—George Santayana

George had decided to add an element to the garden that would highlight the pivotal connection that existed between pollinating insects and flowering plants. By far, his favorite winged pollinator was the monarch butterfly. After just a little research online in the reading and game room, he was alarmed that the monarch population in North America was estimated to have declined by as much as 80 percent over the past decade. The acknowledged subject matter expert, Dr. Lincoln Brower, ironically had just passed away himself, and in a way, this spurred George into action, not that he ever needed much encouragement. Brower taught at Amherst and the University of Florida and had dedicated six decades to the study of monarchs and most recently attached his name to a petition to list the monarch as an endangered species. George trusted scientific research to guide intelligent environmental policy, and if Brower had said there was a problem, then there was a problem. This mighty pollinator, which was as light as a paper clip, migrated like birds or whales, as far as two thousand miles from different US states and Canada to the mountains of Mexico and the California coast. One of the problems was the destruction of its primary food source and breeding site, the humble milkweed plant. This ubiquitous plant could be found along the ditches of two-lane highways up, down, and across the US, which facilitated the epic trips taken by monarchs to their winter habitats. Decades earlier, many county and state governments began using strong herbicides (e.g., Monsanto's Roundup) to kill vegetation along these roads to save on the cost of mowing, which began wiping out the monarch's food source. Equally as challenging were the more recent drastic swings in both hot and cold temperatures brought on by what most science-believing people labeled as human-created climate change. George had no doubt that this was real, and while he acknowledged his own impotence in fighting the forces at play in this battle on a worldwide scale, he did believe in his own small world he could make a difference. Plus, to his way of thinking, he really believed that he had never seen anybody not react with a smile to the presence of a monarch butterfly. Thus, the idea of a large butterfly garden and habitat on the backside of the courtyard was born.

Several weeks earlier, in midspring, George had taken a delivery of fifty two-gallon potted milkweed plants from his favorite nursery supplier just outside Hidden Falls. He had quietly placed them in a cleared section on the perimeter of the courtyard garden with a six-foot-square cleared space in the middle. Extending out from the square, he staggered twenty-five milkweed plants in each direction, with a tidy vermiculite path bordering the space. With moderate watering every other day, the plants were beginning to sprout their first small orange-and-red blooms, which just the day before had begun to attract the first monarchs. He watched this day as females landed on many of his plants and turned their bodies up to the underside of the leaves to deposit the small white orb, which was the egg that would net a yellow-and-black caterpillar in a few days. As the caterpillars began to eat the leaves of their respective host plant, George anxiously awaited the arrival of his new screened habitat, which would serve as the nursery for chrysalis formation. While the caterpillars could and did form into chrysalises in a natural setting, by placing them on plants inside a habitat, the yield to butterfly was much greater by eliminating predators like birds and rodents, who fed on the mature, nutrient-rich caterpillars. Plus, watching a butterfly emerge from the chrysalis and then releasing it off one's hand into the air was as close to a spiritual moment that a human could have, as far as George was concerned. With any luck, in about three weeks, he would begin experiencing that moment, which he would gladly share with any of his "fellow inmates" who wanted to participate.

As he was thinking about that prospect, Emmaline and Suzanne appeared and asked him what he was up to. Just then, one of the monarchs landed softly on Suzanne's head. She was delighted, but Emmaline was much less enthusiastic as she backpedaled to a safe distance. Suzanne said she had never had a butterfly visit her before, and it was a magical experience. George explained the scope of his full plans and that with any luck, the courtyard would soon be inhabited by lots of monarchs. Emmaline commented that as long as they didn't land directly on her, she found the whole thing very serene, which George decided was as close to an endorsement as he would get from her. He remembered one year earlier when a volunteer had started to show up with a very friendly golden retriever therapy dog, which three members of the Vera Bradley Bridge Mafia said left hair on their slacks and deposited brown "land mines" in the courtyard. He would create a low-key butterfly garden and habitat in hopes of a better outcome.

20

Life Moves On With or Without You

Fate is never fair. You are caught in a current much stronger than you are; struggle against it and you'll drown not just yourself but those who try to save you. Swim with it and you'll survive.

—Cassandra Clare

Anna was in her office lamenting about not being able to surface any viable candidates to replace her when her cell chimed. She saw that it was Dr. MacDonald and picked it up.

"Hi, Ian. How was your half day yesterday with Dr. Washington?" she asked.

"I could tell you it was good, but it wouldn't be doing it justice. He may be the smartest and most insightful person I have had the good fortune to spend time with. In about two hours, he dissected my practice's challenges and gave me a road map on how to begin the fix. Truly remarkable. His suggestions on staffing were spot-on, including the recommendation to make a change that I would like your perspective on. He picked up on Beverly's apparent unhappiness and gruff manner with just about everyone and doesn't think she should be retained. I believe he is right. He also recommended that you have probably dealt with exiting staff and might have some insight into the best way to get it done."

"He recognized exactly what I did with my first encounter with Beverly. She needs to go, Ian, and the sooner the better. My advice is to set up a meeting, have Cindy present to witness the exchange, and simply state that your expectations for her position have changed and the practice will be moving forward without her. Give her two weeks' severance and move on. In the interim, get a temp in to answer the phone, greet patients, and keep some semblance of order in the office. She will object, and you need to listen and then simply say you no longer need her services. Dr. Washington probably advised you to check with one of the law practices in your building to cover your bases, and if not, I would do that as well."

"Thanks, Anna. That all makes great sense. One more quick question. You wouldn't happen to know who I should contact to identify a strong jack-of-all-trades type to join our office staff, would you?"

"I don't, Ian, but if I had the same need, the first person I would check with would be Bonnie, my right hand, who stays close with the

Hidden Valley Community College staff. I can loop her in if that would help," offered Anna.

"Tell her I will be in contact and generally what it is about. I owe you, Anna, and I'm not sure how to return the favor," Dr. MacDonald replied.

"We'll figure something out, my friend," Anna reassured.

*

Anna decided she should keep Angela in the loop about her dad and sent her a quick message requesting a callback when time allowed. Not surprisingly, her cell chirped ten minutes later with Angela on the other end.

"So tell me what kind of havoc my cantankerous but lovable father is creating out in the hinterlands of Wisconsin."

"I have nothing but good news, girl. He is out of his room about 50 percent of the time during the day. He has continued to charm the other residents with another impromptu concert, this time with some Dave Brubeck. As I think you know, he made a very helpful suggestion regarding the room placement of one of our residents, which has calmed that resident considerably. He is spending time with that resident, with whom he shares a passion for baseball and a passing acquaintance with a legendary player, Satchel Paige. He has spoken with the patient's daughter and reassured her that she made a good decision to place him here. Our resident rowdy, George Binson, who doubles as our groundskeeper, has become a good friend of your dad's, and he is schooling Elijah on all things green. Lastly, he spent a half-day with one of Hidden Falls' new primary-care-practice docs and gave him sage counsel regarding personnel and practice management.

"I think he needs to come to grips with the loss of your mom a bit more, and Dr. Penelope Lipscombe, our contract psychologist, agrees. He is progressing nicely and will probably be ready to come home in a couple of weeks or a month at the most. To be honest, I'm delighted with his improvement but a little sad at the prospect of not having him here. He's contributing so much," finished Anna.

"I can't say I am surprised. You have built quite a wonderful facility that contributes so much to all the lucky residents who land there. What I know about my dad is that he absolutely thrives when he has a purpose. For him, that primary purpose has been the well being of others and the sharing of wisdom that has been shared so generously with him. Oddly, Serenity Acres has reawakened those things in him and consequently brought him back from a dark place. I will leave it to you to figure out when to send him back south to his former life."

"It will be my pleasure, Angela," replied Anna with the glimmer of a crazy idea beginning to germinate in her very creative mind.

21

Games of Chance Are Designed to Test Our Fundamental Intelligence and Our Self-Control.

Some luck lies in not getting what you thought you wanted but getting what you have, which, once you have it, you may be smart enough to see is what you would have wanted had you known.

—Garrison Keillor

Everyone had been talking about the annual trip to the Ho-Chunk Indian casino in Black River Falls for a couple of weeks. Fortunes were going to be won and lost mostly through copious amounts of handle pulling at the nickel slots. The previous year, apparently, Sarah Wilson had scored a jackpot worth several hundred dollars and promptly spent the whole thing on dinner at Dairy Queen for the whole bus on the way home, laying waste to the idea that people who owned banks were good with their money. This year, they had chartered a larger bus with leather seats, Wi-Fi, and its own powder room for the trip. Thirty-four were scheduled to make the trip this year, which was an all-day affair sure to produce multiple adventures with accompanying vivid accounts.

Dr. Washington was easily convinced to join the group for the outing to Black River Falls. He had spent time there back in the early '90s consulting with the Ho-Chunk health-care committee on how best to set up clinics to serve their population in Wisconsin. The committee was made up of leaders from the various Ho-Chunk tribes, and it was chaired by a young college graduate who was a product of the educational support program of the Ho-Chunk Nation of Wisconsin. Now Elijah was going to one of the flagship casinos that made all these wonderful infrastructure programs possible to have fun and meet with his old friend Dr. Robert Redfeather, who was in fact that young college graduate from the health-care committee and now the president of the Ho-Chunk Nation of Wisconsin. While they had corresponded infrequently in the interim, this would be the first time they had been together since 1994. Elijah thought, *Funny how quickly twenty-six years can pass when it seems pretty much like yesterday that it happened.*

The atmosphere inside the luxury coach was similar to a family road trip vacation from the early 1960s. Lots of discussion and laughing, with the occasional question shouted over a couple of rows of seats and answered in a raised voice so that all were privy to the conversation. About a half hour in, George leaned into the aisle and asked Sarah

Wilson if she was buying dinner on the way home again, and if so, could they elevate the choice of restaurant. Sarah, in the spirit of the road trip, stated that she would have to move her game to the blackjack table from the nickel slots and luck into a hot streak, which was not at all out of the question. As to the dining upgrade, she would consider the request if all agreed to a reasonable ceiling on the entrée and only one cocktail. George replied, "May the Force be with you, my dear," which received a few chuckles and a few questions about what "the Force" was.

Upon arrival at the Black River Falls Casino at about 10:30 in the morning, a handsome group of casino staff was at the entrance with a sign that read "Welcome Back, Serenity Acres!"

Emmaline, Suzanne, Verna, and Sarah were the first off the bus, and Emmaline said to Suzanne, "We must have contributed more last year than I'd estimated."

Suzanne replied, "No, dear, this is just a very well-run place with nice owners."

As Elijah stepped off the bus, a tall, distinguished man in a tailored blue suit with a turquoise-adorned belt buckle and a well-groomed salt-and-pepper ponytail stepped forward. He displayed a broad grin and grasped Elijah's hand firmly.

"Dr. Washington, welcome to Black River Falls on behalf of a grateful Ho-Chunk Nation," beamed Robert Redfeather.

Elijah smiled as he took in the powerful figure in front of him and said, "Dr. Redfeather, I am honored that you would take time out of your busy day to greet me."

"Come inside, my friend. You are the highlight of my day, and we need to sit and catch up after so many years."

Robert led Elijah into the casino and up a short flight of stairs to a mezzanine area with lounge chairs and tables overlooking the gaming floor. "Sit, please, and what may we bring you to drink?" asked Robert.

"Black coffee would be great," replied Elijah.

The waitress returned quickly to their reserved table and left coffee and a glass of iced tea.

Elijah waited for Robert to speak as he looked out over the already busy main gaming area of the casino.

Finally, Dr. Redfeather turned and told Dr. Washington, "When I sit here in my current position, it is like gazing out over an enterprise that sustains all the members of our tribe. It is ironic that the profits come primarily from our white brothers and sisters and from the sale of alcohol, two of the things that almost destroyed us. Maybe it's just the gods fixing things in their own way. Who knows? A lot has happened since we were together the last time. What was it—1994? I went back to school with a scholarship provided by the tribe and finished my doctorate in public administration at the U in Madison. I came back to Black River and went to work for our development arm. Six casinos later, we have a sustainable source of income for all our infrastructure investments. Education, housing, health care in all their facets take up almost 79 percent of our income, and I would like that percentage to increase. Administrative overhead is roughly 13.5 percent, and the remainder is invested in development, welfare, and local government services.

"I was initially hesitant to run for office within the community, but several elders reminded me that it was why my people had invested in me. How do you argue with that? So here I am—hopefully the kind of enlightened leader that makes a contribution to those that have cared for him." He stopped and waited comfortably in the silence for Elijah to reply.

"Well, the intervening years have been pretty good to me as well, until recently. My practice gradually began to consume less and less of my time as I became involved with medical management responsibilities at the hospital. Between those duties and various board positions around the city, my time delivering hands-on patient care dwindled to about two days a week. My daughter is thriving as the medical director of the Northwestern ER, and I was pretty much coasting along comfortably until three months ago. My beautiful wife, Sandra, died suddenly, and my world no longer held my interest. I became a hermit in my house, pretty much quit eating, and was finally rescued by my daughter, who shipped me off to her friend's long-term-care facility over in Hidden Falls. I hated it for the first couple of days but then began to watch the residents live and laugh with each other. A nice young psychologist coaxed my head out of my ass just enough for me to venture outside my room, and to be honest, I really like the people and the place. In all candor, I'm not sure where that leaves me, but for right now, just engaging with life—any life—is a step forward."

They sat comfortably for a few minutes, and then Dr. Redfeather made Dr. Washington an interesting proposition. It so happened that the Ho-Chunk health-care authority was embarking on the next phase of its development; it was going to explore its inpatient contracts, wellness programs, and child health deliverables and was forming a committee to work through the process. Robert wondered if Elijah might like to participate as one of the medical experts on the panel. Elijah surprised himself by immediately saying he would be honored, realizing that he was indeed tiptoeing back into the world of the functioning.

*

Down on the casino floor, the Serenity Acres crew was doing their damn best to keep the Ho-Chunk Nation more than solvent. The nickel slots had definitely lived up to their reputation as one-armed bandits, liberating several hundred dollars from the would-be fortune seekers from Hidden Falls. The good news was that everyone was still having a jolly good time and showed no signs of quitting anytime soon. Seeing this, Elijah wandered into the somewhat empty cocktail lounge off the main floor and noticed the Steinway grand sitting covered over in the corner. He strolled over to the bench, lifted the cover, and hit middle C, which sounded right. Immediately, the bartender came out from behind the bar to discourage Elijah, but before he could get Elijah's attention, he was waylaid by Dr. Redfeather, who whispered something in his ear, which exacted a nod and a walk back to behind the bar. Robert walked over and helped Elijah pull off the cover and folded it behind the piano.

He said, “Sinatra,” and then walked back and sat at the bar with another iced tea.

Elijah adjusted the bench to put the pedals where he wanted them and then launched into a smooth jazz version of Sinatra standards. “Witchcraft,” “Summer Wind,” “When Somebody Loves You,” “All or Nothing at All,” “Night and Day,” “You’ll Never Know,” “Time After Time,” “Begin the Beguine,” “Day by Day,” and “People Will Say We’re in Love” rolled smoothly out of the piano, with the bar patrons stopping conversation to enjoy his mastery of the keys.

When Dr. Redfeather strolled over to the bar, the bartender told him that they needed hire this guy if they could afford him.

Robert replied, “Just signed him up a while ago,” and he winked at Elijah.

*

Elsewhere on the floor, someone was indeed hot at the blackjack table, but it wasn’t Sarah Wilson. June Wilhelm, who had been on fire for the better part of an hour and had a stack of chips in front of her, asked the dealer how far up she was.

The dealer eyed the pile and said about $5,000. June said, "Thanks, I'm done, and here's fifty for your trouble. Which way is the cashier?" She walked calmly over to the cashier and exchanged the chips for cash and signed the receipt / tax form. She then threaded her arm through George's and said, "I am buying you a drink, Mr. Binson. Please escort me to the nearest bar."

George replied, "This way, madam, and may I say you are quite the blackjack player."

"You can't judge a book by its cover, George. Lead on," replied June.

In the cocktail lounge, June spotted Elijah and Robert together at the bar and headed over with George in tow.

Elijah inquired how she did, and George shouted, "She broke the fucking bank!"

June chuckled and showed the wad of cash to Elijah and Robert. Elijah introduced Dr. Redfeather and explained his role with the Ho-Chunk Nation. June seemed a bit embarrassed, and before she could apologize for winning, Robert assured her that it was good for patrons to do well and let others know, intimating that the house certainly won far more than it lost. Visibly relieved, she then asked Robert if there was a good pizza place to order pizzas to go in Black River Falls. He said indeed there was. Right down the street was Francesco's, which had been there for more than thirty years. She asked for the number and calmly dialed and ordered five extra-large cheese, five extra-large meat lovers, and five extra-large vegetarians, with enough napkins and paper plates to accommodate thirty-five diners for pick up at 5:00 p.m.

Then she turned to Robert and asked where the closest package store was. Robert replied, "Right across the street from the pizza parlor."

"Thanks, Dr. Redfeather. That will do quite nicely," stated June.

*

As the crew climbed on the bus at the appointed 4:45 p.m. departure time, June waited until they were all seated, then asked the driver for the microphone for a quick announcement.

"Dear fellow residents and gamblers. I hope everyone had as much fun as I did today. Lady Luck was at my side at the blackjack table, and I won several thousand dollars. In celebration, I have taken the liberty of ordering pizzas from what is purported to be the best joint in town, conveniently located across the street from a package store, which I have confirmed carries Leinenkuegel's, shandies, and assorted soft drinks. It's on me! Lastly, I am intending to take the remainder of the cash and start a fund for a down payment for a house for Melanie, Samantha, and their new arrival. We can't have those precious people starting life as a family in a one-bedroom apartment, can we?"

Silence settled over the bus until Emmaline stood in a very un-Emmaline fashion and shouted loudly, "Three cheers for June!" and the bus rocked with the response.

Elijah thought again how blessed he was to have landed in the middle of this wonderful group of people.

22

Mysteries of the Mind

"Sometimes," he sighed, "I think the things I remember are more real than the things I see."

—Arthur Golden, *Memoirs of a Geisha*

Some things seemed to move quickly at Serenity Acres. Just two days after the trip to Black River Falls and the casino, the Samantha/Melanie house fund had grown from just under $4,000 to more than $30,000, thanks largely to the generosity of Emmaline Yoder, Verna Winstadt, Sarah Wilson, and more than ten other residents. With the reasonable price of very nice housing in Hidden Falls, everyone was confident that they were on the verge of providing a down payment for a wonderful starter home for the couple and their soon-to-arrive baby.

Dr. Washington had been continuing his daily "conversations" with Edgar Vornoy and had noticed at least a change in Edgar's eye movements when he discussed certain topics. The hot buttons seemed to be his daughter, Daphne, and his baseball career, especially any reference to Satchel Paige. Elijah was curious if Edgar's dementia had an organic cause, like the insidious beta-amyloid plaque buildup in the brain, the hallmark of Alzheimer's, or whether it was the common standard late-onset dementia caused by vascular deficiencies in the brain. The treatment and drug options can and do overlap, but being as specific as possible when identifying the likely cause can help in interfacing most effectively with the patient. Dr. Washington realized that he was definitely using his medical skills again, and it not only didn't bother him, it felt right. He would contact Daphne later and ask if Edgar had a specific diagnosis for his deteriorating mental state prior to admission. One thing for sure was that any mention of either Satchel Paige or Daphne evoked a response that outwardly appeared to be not just recognition but happiness as well. Elijah would be sure to share that with Daphne when they spoke.

*

Anna had not had any luck with Med List in surfacing an administrator candidate, and the time frame to get it done was shortening quickly. Interestingly, just as she was mulling over how to find just the right person, Dr. Washington poked his head into her office and asked if she had a moment.

Anna said, "Of course," and motioned to one of the guest chairs in front of her desk.

Elijah asked if it was OK to contact Daphne and inquire about any testing Edgar may have had prior to admission. He offered that in his experience, patients with different forms of dementia responded differently, and knowing what their dementia type was could help tailor not only interactions but care plans.

Anna looked at him quietly for a moment. "Dr. Washington, your abilities and knowledge are impressive and deep; I knew that on paper when you got here and from my friendship with your daughter. However, I must say I have met other medical staff who are boarded in multiple specialties but lack the most important thing you possess in abundance: a caring, curious and generous spirit. Without consulting Dr. Lipscombe, I can say with some certainty that you have beaten the depression you arrived here with, and I take great pride and pleasure from being a small part of that healing." She then asked what needed to be asked. "So what's next for Dr. Elijah Washington? You are too capable and engaged to completely hang up your spurs, and it seems to me that it would be a huge waste of a resource if you did. You are welcome to stay as long as you like. You know that we like low-maintenance residents who can afford retail. In fact, your demographic is right in the Silver Age profiling sweet spot. What are your plans?" Anna paused.

After about ten seconds, Dr. Washington said, "Thanks for your kind words, and yes, I am not in the pathetic state I was just a few weeks ago. Between Cookie's food, the wonderful company of the other residents, and you and your staff, I have indeed rejoined the ranks of the living. As to my immediate plans, I have just started to consider them. Quite frankly, I agree with you that I do need to utilize my background to make a contribution somewhere. In confidence, I'm not sure that somewhere is back in Chicago. While I treasure everything about the city, there are now so many ghosts for me there that a change of venue might be appropriate.

"Interestingly, I just accepted a consulting role with the Ho-Chunk health-care committee in Black River Falls offered by my friend Dr. Robert Redfeather, the president of the Ho-Chunk people. My commitment to you is that I will not stay here for longer than another couple of weeks. I haven't even had this conversation with Angela yet, so if you speak to her, let's keep this between the two of us."

"Rest assured that this is absolutely considered privileged information, Dr. Washington. Also, if you don't mind, I may have a few suggestions for your future professional plans. And by all means, please contact Daphne and inquire about Edgar's diagnostic info," said Anna.

After Elijah had left her office, Anna sat quietly for a moment with the Med List job description and qualification guidelines and thought, *Am I being crazy, or could the answer to our leadership needs here at Serenity Acres have been staying with us for the last month or so? Who do I trust enough to vet this past who knows this operation and me well enough to say either, 'Great idea,' or ask if I'm off my meds? Dr. MacDonald, of course.*

23

Tell Me I'm Crazy, I Dare You

Fear is the lack of faith in one's ability to create powerful solutions.

—T. F. Hodge

Dr. Angela Washington's life continued to be consumed by the job she loved at the Northwestern ER. Sending her father north to be tended to by her close friend Anna Halstead and her expert staff had been a gift from God. She felt guilty that she had not been back up to Hidden Falls to check on her dad, but her text messages to and from him had signaled an emergence from his funk, and her calls with Anna had reinforced that impression. The other reason for her guilt was she had not even shared with her father a new and very positive development in her personal life.

Right after she had taken the senior Dr. Washington to his current spot in Wisconsin, she had attended a board meeting of the The Art Institute of Chicago and met a new board member. His name was Tobias Galloway, and he was a handsome black architect who had been immediately attracted to Angela, which had both surprised and delighted her. Since their initial meeting, they had not spent longer than two days without making time to have lunch, dinner, visit a music venue, or just walk and talk. At thirty-seven and with an unapologetic commitment to a job she loved, Angela had pretty much accepted that she would be a single, successful, professional woman who found fulfillment in her life with things other than a man. Now Toby had pretty much turned that idea on its head, and while she was more than nervous about it, she had fully embraced the vision of a far different future that included him.

Tobias Galloway was from the DC Metro area, where his father was a very prominent lawyer with one of the big national firms that specialized in representing large corporate clients and lobbying on their behalf. His mother, like Angela's, had given up an early career in teaching to support her husband through law school and then stay home to raise Tobias and his sister. Without specifically articulating the similarities of their backgrounds and upbringings, they recognized and appreciated how close it made them in such a rapid fashion. Tobias had been a fairly good high school basketball player at an elite prep school outside of DC, and at his father's suggestion, he had leveraged that to get a scholarship to the Massachusetts Institute of Technology to study architecture, which had been his passion since childhood. He achieved academic All-American status as a basketball player and was grateful that it afforded him the opportunity to pursue his career ambition as an architect at one of the top-three programs in the country. After obtaining his master's in architecture, he was more than ready to join the workforce and immediately set his sights on working for one of the elite firms in Chicago, the generally acknowledged center for American architecture.

Chicago is widely credited with development of the steel frame structure design that made possible the idea of skyscrapers. Additionally, Frank Lloyd Wright, Louis Sullivan, Ludwig Mies van der Rohe, and Holabird & Root, some of the fathers of American architecture, all made Chicago their home. Consequently, iconic buildings abound in the Windy City and pull strongly on the imagination and desire of aspiring young architects. Tobias, with his college résumé, had landed not unexpectedly at one the premier firms with offices right in the middle of the Loop, where he was thriving.

While Angela had shared more with Tobias than she had with any other male acquaintance, she had not divulged that her father owned and lived in one of the most famous homes in the Chicago area. To her way of thinking, that would have been bragging or trying to impress, which she had been taught her entire life was boorish behavior. At some point, that fact would come out, and he would likely be more impressed that she hadn't tried to win him with things but simply by sharing herself.

So when Anna called Angela and said she wanted to give her an update on her father, she was anxious to return the call not only to find out how Elijah was faring but also to share her personal news with someone she was close to.

Anna picked up her cell immediately and started with the good news. "Well, Angela, your father has not only improved remarkably but has quickly become a vital part of the fabric here at Serenity Acres. Seems the key to his recovery was his own inability to cease applying his knowledge and wisdom in the assistance of others. Penelope Lipscombe picked up on it first when he performed his unsolicited environmental assessment on one of our patients. Since then, he has befriended not only that patient but also his daughter, who is more grateful than you could imagine. He also has become close to one of our new community family practice doctors, who is relying on Elijah for practice, personnel, and life advice. The long and short of it is he doesn't have time any longer to dwell on his own issues. Who would have thought that people throwing themselves into their work could be so therapeutic?"

Angela laughed and said, "Up until recently, that was my whole life strategy. I am so, so grateful for what you have done for my father. On a different topic, I wanted to share something a bit more personal about me. Out of nowhere, a wonderful man has tumbled into my life! Tobias Galloway is a successful architect, and we share so much in common that since my dad has been gone, we have been together almost daily, sometimes hourly. I'm so busy I really don't have a lot of friends to share this with, and I need to or I might just pop. You are the lucky one that gets to know first. Listen to me! I'm like a giddy teenager."

"That is better than great, Angela! I can't wait to meet him. The other thing I should mention about your dad is that I think he is pretty close to moving on with his life, and he has articulated that to me pretty directly. My opinion is that he could use your guidance as he navigates the next section of his journey. If you can, I would plan on sitting down with him sooner than later to provide counsel as he figures out his next move," offered Anna.

Angela thanked her again profusely and promised she would be in contact with Elijah.

Anna smiled as she hung up with Angela and thought she had some work to do. Time to begin to validate her succession plan.

24

I Figured Out a Way You Can Pay Me Back

> Well, I always know what I want. And when you know what you want—you go toward it. Sometimes you go very fast, and sometimes only an inch a year. Perhaps you feel happier when you go fast. I don't know. I've forgotten the difference long ago, because it really doesn't matter, so long as you move.
>
> —Ayn Rand, *We the Living*

"Ian, what are you doing for lunch today? I haven't been downtown in Hidden Falls for a couple of months and need a break midday. I'll buy at the Nook Café on the square at whatever time you can make it. I need to bounce something off you. What say you?" Anna hit Send, and the text flew off into the ether to Dr. MacDonald.

Ian texted back that he never refused a free lunch from his favorite nursing home administrator and noon would work if he could talk with his mouth full and be back in his office by 12:45. Anna shot back the a thumbs-up emoji followed by, "SYT." That gave her the midmorning for a walkabout, which brought on a brief feeling of melancholy knowing that she wouldn't be doing them much longer. Then, in normal Anna fashion, she told herself to look forward to all the other new adventures ahead and remove her head from her ass. With that attitude, she stopped by the nursing station and spied Melanie and Samantha in a brief joyful embrace, who both looked like the cat that swallowed the canary. With a suspicion of what the news might be, she approached the two with a quiet and expectant look.

It paid off when Melanie and Samantha pulled her aside and said almost breathlessly, "We're expecting! Got the call just now, and it seems that Sam is indeed a fertile young thing. The procedure took on the first try. I'm going to cry!" whimpered Melanie.

There was a long group hug between the three with a mixture of snuffles and giggles that left little doubt to anyone nearby what it was about.

"You are going to have to share this quickly here at the ranch. Following the first-ever fertility symposium, you are both aware that you have nearly a hundred honorary grandmothers- and grandfathers-in-waiting here. Congratulations!" added Anna.

*

Following a slow and gratifying stroll through A and B wings and ending in the dining room, Anna pulled Cookie aside and asked in a hushed tone, "As our resident expert on all things culinary, what do pregnant women crave the most?"

Without skipping a beat, Cookie said, "I knew it. Those two positively glowed this morning when I saw them. The answer to your question is, absolutely anything, but the iconic offering would be ice cream and dill pickles. I will crank up the ice-cream maker after lunch. Can you grab some big fat kosher dills somewhere?"

"Headed to town for a lunch meeting and will stop by the deli on the way back here with a whole jar in hand," guaranteed Anna.

*

Anna arrived early at the Nook Café and grabbed a booth for two in the back corner. Five minutes late and at almost a dead run, Dr. MacDonald busted through the front door, and the owner, Mildred, in the kitchen behind the pass-through window, called, "Hi, Doc!" as he headed toward Anna.

"Sit down and slow down, Ian. If they served beer, I would have had a cold one waiting for you. How's it going?" asked Anna.

Ian laughed and said, "And I would probably have picked it up and drained it. It's actually going quite well, thanks to Dr. Washington, you, and Bonnie. The kind of busy we are experiencing now is the good kind. I contacted the Hidden Falls Community College and spoke with Bonnie's friend, who gave me the name of last year's top graduate in the accounting/bookkeeping associate's program. She had been hired at the local office of one of the national tax preparation outfits. After about two minutes of describing what I had in mind for the office manager position, the practice management software we were using, and the potential for growth in the job, she asked if she could come and see me on her break that afternoon. She has been with us for a week, we are about a hundred times more organized than we had been, she smiles and asks for more every day, and the second day, she showed me how the billing feature of our MedConnection practice management system had not even been activated. Now that it has, our insurance claims are almost caught up, and our patient portion receivables are miraculously starting to run smoothly as well. So if I seem harried and distracted, it's only because we are cleaning up several years' worth of poor business practices. But as the saying goes, I can see the light at the end of the tunnel and am moderately confident that it's not an oncoming train."

The waitress showed up, and Ian said, "Bring us two specials," checking visually if Anna was OK with that, which she was, having seen the billboard announcing the special on the way in as a grilled ham and cheese with a Waldorf side salad.

They chatted for just a few minutes and out came the two specials with a Coke and an iced tea. Ian offered Anna either of the drinks (she grabbed the Coke), and he then said, "So what's up?"

"Do you remember when you called me and vetted Dr. Washington's observations and recommendations? Well, I need to run something by you that I am considering and would value your opinion as to whether I am brilliant or a candidate for serious therapy of some kind," said Anna.

Ian smiled and reassured, "Well, I am pretty confident that therapy is not in your future, so lay it on me, partner."

"I am going to share somewhat confidential information with you regarding Elijah and trust you will understand why when I explain my idea. As you know from interfacing with him, he has certainly progressed from the depressive state he found himself in when he arrived. Penelope's prescription of engagement with others as the best therapy proved prescient. From his recommendations on Edgar Vornoy, to his reassurance of his daughter, to his rapid integration with his fellow residents, to his willing and sage advice to you, to his calm and generous interface with all the Serenity team, including me, he has pretty much realized he is not done contributing in some fashion to the health-care community. He has accepted an invitation by the president of the Ho-Chunk Nation of Wisconsin to consult once again with their tribal health-care committee as they look forward for more improvements, which will meet up at their headquarters in Black River Falls. While he has had an incredible career in Chicago, I think his next contribution might just be up here in Wisconsin. You know I am leaving at the beginning of the school year, and we have candidly come up dry to this point looking for my replacement. So here is my out-of-the-box crazy idea. With his permission, I want to put Elijah forth as a candidate for administrator of Serenity Acres. No one knows about this but you. There. I said it. What do you think?"

Dr. MacDonald put down his fork, wiped his mouth with his napkin, and said, "If this were a case study and the primary question was whether a resident in treatment could be considered for a leadership position where they are being treated, the answer would probably be no. But it's not a hypothetical situation; it involves two remarkable people. First, there is you, who molded a good nursing home facility into a community of love, care, and success for residents and staff. Don't think about arguing with me until I'm done. Both in financial and quality performance, Serenity Acres is at the top not only in Wisconsin but also within the entire Silver Age community. I know; I've checked on the 'google machine,' as my mother calls it. Secondly, the candidate in question is not just some midseventies depressive patient who randomly landed in your care. He is perhaps the most distinguished medical practitioner in one of America's premier health-care markets who brings with him a host of not only medical expertise but management, ethical, and life experience as well. If there is the slightest possibility that he would consider taking the helm at Serenity, not pursuing that would be abandoning the future of all that you have worked so hard to build and, in my world, be labeled malpractice. So no, Anna, you aren't crazy or off your meds. How can I help?"

25

Are You Sure About This, Pop?

I don't see why there should be a point where everyone decides you're too old. I'm not too old, and until I decide I'm too old, I'll never be too fucking old.

—Lemmy Kilmister, a.k.a. Ian Fraser Willis, lead singer and bass guitarist of Motörhead

With a sense of both excitement and trepidation—two emotions that pair themselves often—Tobias drove Angela up to Hidden Falls to have lunch with her father and discuss his immediate future. She assured him that her father would not consider meeting him for the first time and talking about his own personal plans awkward. Tobias thought that he would never be that confident or self-assured and this was indeed going to be an interesting day. He was also excited about driving his new Lincoln MKX on the highway for the first time, despite the ribbing Angela had given him about going all Matthew McConaughey weird on her. He defended himself by claiming he bought his new ride in spite of the strange commercials, not because of them. Angela laughed at that and accepted his response as rational. She had to admit that both the ride and interior of the Lincoln were comparable if not superior to her Porsche—and at half the cost.

"So, Angela, give me just a little insight into what you expect out of this visit. Are you looking to influence your father or just to determine where his head is and what he has planned?" asked Tobias.

With a chuckle, Angela responded, "Once you spend time with Elijah Washington, you will understand that influencing him is not something that is done over a lunch. He is deliberative to a fault, and the deliberation is based on years of experience and reliance on those he admires or respects. We are just going to bear witness to the great man's planned new chapter."

"You seem comfortable with that. Doesn't bother you at all that he is making these kinds of decisions without your input?" asked Tobias honestly.

"Toby, I've watched this guy accomplish, teach, mentor, and contribute more to the organizations and people he has been involved with than absolutely anyone I know. In that context, why would it bother me?"

"We really have had similar life experiences. He sounds just like my father. Tell me the truth. Do you ever resent the shadow he casts?" Toby offered.

"Hell no. I appreciate being one of the recipients of his wisdom!" Angela chirped.

"Now that is a high compliment. I am truly looking forward to meeting this guy."

It was Saturday, and the traffic thinned out as they left the northern suburbs of Chicago and headed almost straight north to Hidden Falls. The Wisconsin countryside was lush and beautiful with woods, farms, barns, fields, streams, and numerous signs indicating proximity to loads of lakes. The vast majority of the lakes had Native American–sounding names, giving a real sense of what the land must have been like a few hundred years earlier. While foreign to the two city dwellers speeding north, it was truly eye candy that promoted a silent but pleasant outing.

The three-hour drive further cemented Angela's feelings for Tobias. They could talk about personal things with complete candor or just enjoy the silence. Either was most pleasant, and she realized that she had never experienced this with another man and hoped like hell their lunch with her father was a success. She was about to find out as they hit the city limits sign for Hidden Falls and headed toward Serenity Acres. They turned into the visitors parking area, looked at each other, laughed, and then headed for the entrance.

Anna was right inside the door, having warned Bonnie that she wanted a heads-up as soon as she spotted a nice car with an Illinois plate pull into the parking lot.

Anna broke the ice with a declaration. "Welcome, Angela and Mr. Galloway, to the best nursing and convalescent home in the great state of Wisconsin. Let's go find Dr. Washington."

"Heard a lot of wonderful things about you, Anna, and please call me Tobias or Toby."

She liked him instantly and gave Angela a huge hug. "I think I know where he is, from the beautiful sounds coming from the reading and game room. Let's go see," encouraged Anna.

After a short stroll down the hall and into the R&G room, they indeed found Elijah playing excerpts from *The Four Seasons* by Vivaldi to a mesmerized audience of twenty-five or so residents. Toby immediately took a chair and sat in uninhibited awe as the sound flowed from the piano with such precision and ease that it could have been a recording. Angela stood behind him with tears in her eyes as she remembered being a little girl asking her dad to play the wedding music, which he informed her was Vivaldi.

Anna put her arm around her friend and told her that this occurred several times a week and always started with Elijah just playing a song and the room slowly filling with appreciative residents. She considered it therapy not only for Dr. Washington but the entire population of Serenity Acres, staff included. Dr. Washington concluded and turned with his normal surprise to see the room occupied by so many music lovers. Unlike the first time he played, he paused and shook hands, chatted, and laughed with the residents. It was a bit like watching him work a room at one of the many board or charity events he'd attended or sponsored over the years. *If there were any doubts about his mental well-being, they have just been erased*, thought Angela.

After a few minutes, Angela took Tobias over and gently tapped her father on the shoulder. He turned and broke into the biggest smile Anna had seen since he'd arrived. He hugged his daughter and turned his attention to the tall young man at her side.

"I am going to assume this nice-looking young fellow is not an Uber driver. Would you care to elaborate, Angela?" quipped Dr. Washington.

"He did give me a ride up here from Chicago, but he is my special new friend, Tobias Galloway. Toby, this is my father, Dr. Elijah Washington," said Angela.

The two men faced off and grasped each other's hands firmly, and Toby offered, "A pleasure to finally meet you, sir, and may I add that your skill on the keys is quite impressive."

"Thanks, Tobias, and what do you say the three of us head over to the Nook Café on the square? They're holding a table and three daily specials for us."

As they walked out of the building to Toby's car, Dr. Washington watched his daughter hold her friend's arm and smile at him warmly.

He thought, *this looks promising*.

Once seated in the back of Toby's new Lincoln, Elijah commented, "This is a nice vehicle. Some people I know seem to prefer overpriced German cars to solid American products. To me, this exudes good judgment and confidence in one's own skin. Don't you think so, Angela?"

"Oh, stop it, Dad. What's in your garage at home?" Angela shot back good-naturedly.

"Gee, I've been gone so long, I can't seem to recall, sweetheart," answered Elijah.

"It's a Bimmer, Dad. A big Bimmer." Angela laughed.

Toby was enjoying the back-and-forth between two people who obviously enjoyed each other's company. Ten minutes later, they pulled up to a parking space directly in front of the Nook Café and walked inside.

*

Mildred saw them come in and yelled from the pass-through window, "Hey, Doc! How are you? Held the booth in the back. Go and sit and turn the reserved sign over. We will be right with you."

Dr. Washington smiled, saluted, and headed for the back with Angela and Toby in tow. He sat across the table from them and took them both in. Without any prejudice, he thought what a handsome couple they were. Then he looked at them and stated, "I'm ordering for us, so don't worry about bothering with the menu. OK, Tobias. I suspect you know a bit about me, and thus, you have me at a distinct disadvantage. So I'll buy lunch if you deliver the CliffsNotes version of your life to this point. Sound fair?"

With that, Toby, in his self-deprecating style, ran Elijah through his parents, childhood, academic background, career, and outside interests—with appropriate positive color commentary from a delighted Angela.

Elijah asked only one question: "Are both your parents still alive?"

"Yes, sir," answered Toby, not knowing what to expect next.

"Stay in close touch and tell them more often than you think you need to how much you appreciate them and love them. Life is short and precious."

"Thank you, sir, for that advice. I think I am fairly good at that, but having it reinforced by someone as wise as you is a nice"

"Angela, he is a winner. What are your intentions?" he asked his daughter with mischief in his smile.

"I recognize that, Dad. Why do you think I conned him into driving me up here today?" She laughed.

The three specials of chicken-fried steak, mashed potatoes and gravy, and a side of corn arrived, and they ordered drinks. On a practical note, Elijah asked Angela if she had been out to his house in Oak Park recently and added that he was pretty sure he had volunteered to host a fund-raiser there for the hospital next month. Angela was suddenly nervous, and—being intuitive—Dr. Washington was pretty confident he knew why. Without hesitating, he asked Tobias if he had been out to the property. Tobias said he had not, but if there was anything he could do to help, he was always available. Before she could stop him, Elijah told Tobias that it would be really helpful to have an architect to consult with about the property because it had historical landmark status, which caused Tobias to ask why.

Very matter-of-factly, Dr. Washington said, "Because it's one of the last Frank Lloyd Wright–designed and –built homes from the second decade of twentieth century. Angela didn't mention that to you?"

After Toby had dropped his fork and Angela had her hands wrapped around her head, Elijah laughed heartily. "I didn't realize our house was such a source of family shame for you, sweetheart. Call me crazy, but my guess is that your architect boyfriend might even consider it somewhat of an upside."

"Dad! What I am I going to do with you?" asked Angela.

"That's the next topic of conversation that I suggest we have over dessert back at the institution. Does that work for both of you?" He was already calling for the check.

26

Is It OK to Be a Little Selfish with Your Future as You Age?

There's nowhere you can be that isn't where you are meant to be.

—John Lennon

They returned to Serenity Acres and headed for the dining room. Dr. Washington asked Cookie if any dessert remained. She told them to find a clean table and she would be right there. They grabbed a table by the french doors that led to the courtyard and watched George working on something. As good as her word, Cookie arrived forthwith carrying three peach cobblers with whipped cream and three forks and told them to enjoy. After the first delicious mouthful, Elijah started his prepared remarks.

"Angela, you know I wasn't pleased with you when you arranged for my stay here. I must now admit that it was either a stroke of genius or a gift from God that brought you to that decision. Needless to say, I was a basket case a few short weeks ago, but thanks to Anna, Penelope, and the staff, my recovery is almost complete. They were patient with me when I arrived, not forcing me into crafts or chair yoga immediately.

They fattened me back up quickly, courtesy of Cookie's culinary magic. Perhaps most significantly, my wonderful fellow residents reminded me that it is indeed possible to face the adversity and the trials of aging with humor and grace, forcing me to ask myself, *If they can handle it this way, what the hell is my problem?* Candidly, I also imagined my beloved wife looking at me and saying, 'Elijah Washington, get on with your life. Since when did you quit or give up when faced with an obstacle? Face the morning with a smile and hope!' So I've decided it is indeed time to move on with my life.

"The question is: Where should that be? My hometown has been so good to me. Great parents, great education, wonderful long marriage, gorgeous and smart daughter, fulfilling career, and more friends than I can count have been my good fortune. The City of Big Shoulders, as Carl Sandberg noted, has indeed given me a full lifetime of memories. But now that it is time to write the last chapter of my life, I feel like I need a new canvas. The smaller, slower, less frantic pace of life here in Hidden Falls feels right to me.

"I have accepted a consulting role with the Ho-Chunk Nation on their health-care committee from my friend Dr. Robert Redfeather. Although he has not offered, I believe that Dr. MacDonald, a new family practice physician here in Hidden Falls, could use some part-time relief occasionally in his busy practice, which would be fun. Lastly, I would really like to volunteer here at Serenity Acres to be with my friends and help in any way I can to get them through Anna's departure, which will be tough on everyone. Not sure for how long, but for right now, I think I would like to make Hidden Falls my home base.

So what do you think?" asked Elijah, looking at both of them.

Without hesitation, Angela replied, "Dad, I'm just happy that you have beaten the blues back. Where you land now is totally up to you, and whatever you decide, you have my support 100 percent. Any ideas on where you might live?"

"Funny you should ask that. I actually have my eye on a second-story loft space above Hayden and Sons True Value right on the square. It's more space than I need, but the old hardwood floors are beautiful, and the acoustics with the eighteen-foot ceilings are magnificent. It would divide into about 1,300 square feet of common room / kitchen and 500 square feet of bedroom/bath. I'm pretty sure the old casement windows are original. Would love to have Toby take a look."

"Well, you have thought this out. Next, you will be telling me what to send from the house," speculated Angela.

"The Steinway, the leather sectional from the front room, my desk in the office, the eight Charles Alston original works, and my entire wardrobe. You can keep or dispose of the rest as you determine what you want to do with the place. I am giving it to you, sweetheart."

After about a full minute of shocked silence, Toby finally added, "Wow! This really was worth the drive."

Elijah roared with laughter and got up and hugged them both, causing Angela to ask, "You are serious, aren't you, Dad?"

"Serious as a heart attack, as your grandfather used to say. Who better to care for the place than the little girl who grew up there who now has access to an in-house architect who probably knows just a little bit about the builder?"

Elijah started to lead them out to the courtyard to introduce them to George, but Angela asked if she could go find Anna to have a quick word before they headed back home. The men waved her off and headed out through the french doors in search of the keeper of the garden.

They found George in the back of the garden in the middle of what had become quite a stand of milkweed plants. As he had told Elijah, he had indeed placed the habitat square in the middle of the space on the little platform he had constructed. It was a five-foot-by-five-foot black metal screen house that he had ordered online and assembled. There were three fairly large potted milkweed plants inside that were literally crawling with the pinkie-sized monarch caterpillars. Hanging from the ceiling were at least twenty light green chrysalises with about another six or seven caterpillars hanging by one end, with the other suspended in the shape of a capital *J*.

George turned, smiled, and said, "This is probably as close as I will come to witnessing the mystery and beauty of the natural world. In another couple of days, the oldest of these chrysalises will magically eject a full-grown monarch butterfly. Then I and any other adventurous souls who wish will take them on our finger, hold them up, and watch as they fly off to make humans smile and flowers bloom. As I told you before, Elijah, every fourth generation makes the great migration, which can be as long as two or three thousand miles. The other three generations live for a couple of weeks, pollinating and laying eggs to continue the species. Generation four has the migration route and the destination of the winter breeding ground programmed into their DNA. Is that fucking cool or what?"

Tobias smiled and looked over at Dr. Washington, who was clearly admiring George's knowledge and work. He thought, *why wouldn't you want to spend time here?* Elijah made George promise that when he thought the first butterfly was going to appear, he would come and get him. They thanked him and headed back toward the building and Angela.

*

Seated in Anna's office, Angela shared what her father had revealed about his plans and was listening to Anna talk about something that, while surprising, was not at all in conflict with what her father had outlined. The only difference was that his role at Serenity Acres would go far beyond that of a volunteer. Anna was clear that this was not her decision alone and that there were several in the chain of command that could put the kibosh on the whole idea. But knowing Anna as she did, she would not bet against her. Once the lady made up her mind, heaven help the human that got in her way.

Later, as Angela and Toby pulled out of Hidden Falls toward the freeway, Toby turned playfully to Angela and asked, "Any more surprises that you would like to spring on me? We've got three hours to fill."

She shook her head and said earnestly, "No, absolutely not, and I apologize for not being more forthcoming about the Oak Park house."

"I have one," said Toby.

"Well, spit it out, young man, as Elijah would say," responded Angela.

"I love you," said Toby without drama.

"Wow, that's a whopper! Do you mind if I ask if the house has anything to do with it?" she said playfully.

"Let's just say it didn't hurt and leave it at that."

They both laughed heartily, and he stopped the car to deliver a long, passionate kiss.

27

Navigating a Treacherous Stretch of Water Takes Skill, Confidence, and the Belief That You Can Do It

A bruise is a lesson … and each lesson makes us better.

George R. R. Martin, *A Game of Thrones*

More than anything else, selling one's house is a sure way to promote action—action with buying another one, action with finding a new job, and in this case, helping to fill the role you are vacating. Sometimes the most unlikely buyers are the quickest and easiest. Soon after the gang at Serenity Acres delivered the down payment gift to Melanie and Samantha, they had rather sheepishly asked if Anna and Tom had sold their house yet. Anna told them not yet, although there were several serious prospective buyers who they were confident were about ready to deliver an offer. Melanie and Samantha were sent to First Farmers Trust Bank by Sarah Wilson with a prearranged appointment with the VP who headed up their mortgage division. He assigned them to a young loan officer who was told by his boss to make it happen. Consequently, the next day, they were approved for slightly more than what the

Halsteads were asking for their vintage craftsman house. They called their real estate agent and put in an offer $2,000 over asking, saying they didn't need to see the house, as they had had dinner or cocktails there about ten times over the previous three years. Anna called Tom, and the deal was sealed within twenty-four hours.

For Anna, she was overjoyed; it was the perfect scenario for all of them. On the other end in, Tom had been working with a real estate agent and was looking at lake properties within fifteen minutes of downtown and Stryker headquarters. He had shown her the three listings he liked the best, and they had agreed on the most expensive, figuring this could be a house that took the girls through high school. After a bit of back-and-forth, they paid a bit over the listing price, rationalizing that Anna's new income would be no lower than that of her current job. So now the only missing piece in the puzzle was filling the administrator's role at Serenity Acres. She knew that others might just give it their best shot, and if it didn't happen, they would be on to the next thing with no regrets. But this place was her pride and joy, and she loved the staff and residents just like family. She was going to deliver the right person to maintain and improve on what she had accomplished, which she knew was a lot. Consequently, her introduction of Dr. Washington to everyone in the decision-making chain at Silver Age was critical and could not be left to chance. The initial screen would be a résumé and phone interview by corporate HR, who were thorough and professional at what they did, thanks to a stellar VP of HR, Susan Scanlon, who reported directly to Kirsten Stanley, the COO, who was a huge fan of Anna's.

After Anna had sprung the idea on Dr. Washington, following her meeting with Angela, she had talked him into letting Bonnie brush up his résumé. He agreed immediately and stated it hadn't been updated in a while, which was an understatement. The educational section and the professional credential pieces were something to read. Bonnie said she didn't know how he was able to get credentialed in four different specialties. He calmly stated time and curiosity. He served on ten different boards, which were split between charities, museums, corporations, and health-care entities. His hobbies were normal (music, reading, art, swimming) until you heard him play the piano and realized he probably embraced each of those with as much intensity as he did his career. The topper was the three references he listed—the president and CEO of Northwestern Health Systems, the president of the Wisconsin Ho-Chunk Nation, and Barack Obama. When asked about the latter, he simply stated he had cared for Michelle's mom, Marian Shields Robinson, and then become friends with the family, gave advice on the ACA, and had attended both inaugurations at their request.

A funny moment occurred when he had asked about his age, and Bonnie had replied that it was indeed one of his strengths. They immediately bonded from that point forward. The phone screen had been conducted by the VP of HR at the direction of the COO, and her only comment was he might be overqualified, which drew chuckles all the way around. So it came to pass that she was charged with setting up the face-to-face with her boss, Bob Struttmeir, VP of the Upper Midwest Region of Silver Age Industries. Mr. Struttmeir had first suggested that Dr. Washington drive down to Des Plaines and they meet at the regional office. Anna had gently pointed out that interviewing the candidate in the setting where he would be working might prove beneficial. Bob finally agreed, and they both knew that time was of the essence, so the next day would be the day, and all those concerned were anxiously awaiting the event.

In the meantime, Elijah was being prepped by the entire staff. Anna had made time with Bonnie, Cookie, Samantha, Melanie, and a few others just for background on their areas, the challenges they faced, and whatever questions Elijah had for each. He learned that the main reason for unexpected time off was problems with childcare, which didn't surprise him. His admiration for Doreen's skills with food grew as she displayed a thorough and thoughtful knowledge of nutritional needs of older adults. He was not surprised when Samantha and Melanie outlined a plan they had for a geri-gym outfitted with equipment that was specifically designed to accommodate seniors and build both aerobic capacity and strength. He assumed that a question from Mr. Struttmeir might involve ideas for innovations—and this last assumption demonstrated how even the most astute could at times be way off the mark.

Having done everything she could think of that would be helpful, Anna asked if Dr. Washington would like to join her, her daughters, Dr. MacDonald, and his wife and son at her house for takeout pizza and drinkable red wine. He responded that he could not think of another way he would prefer to spend the evening. She said she would come and find him around 5:15 when she was done with the day.

They picked up Anna's daughters, Esther and Melissa, from their school, which ran a great and inexpensive summer school program. They got in the middle seat of the van, strapped in, and were introduced to Dr. Washington, who immediately asked them what they had to say for themselves. This was a master stroke of strategy, as Melissa, the second-grader, launched into how disgusting boys were and that one had wiped a large booger on her shirt but the counselor had seen the whole thing and he got a "way long" time-out. At that point, it was fourth-grader Esther's turn to interrogate her mother once again on the new town, lake house, school, and promised boat that Daddy had been talking about. She stated that it had all better be true because they had a lot to make up for moving them to someplace called Kalamazoo, which made Melissa laugh so hard that she farted, which sent the whole van into hysterics. They were saved by their arrival at Luigi's on the square, where Anna picked up three large pizzas and headed toward the house. As soon as they made it through the door, Melissa grabbed Elijah's hand and led him upstairs to her room, which housed the largest collection of stuffed animals this side of the Mississippi, according to her father. She was already planning on adding a whole new group of fish and marine mammals, as they would be living on a lake. Elijah said it sounded like a grand idea.

About ten minutes later, Ian MacDonald, his wife, Erin, and their new son, Eamon, arrived to much fanfare and cooing by all three of the

Halstead females. Paper plates, pizzas, soft drinks, and red wine were all set on the dining room table, and Anna called the group to dinner. Dr. Washington asked if he could offer grace, and Anna indicated that would be great.

"Dear Lord, bless this food to our use and make us ever mindful of the wonderful joy that friends and family bring into our lives. Amen," offered Elijah.

After his usual one glass of red wine and three pieces of pizza, Elijah asked Ian if he had any advice or insights into his interview the next day with Mr. Struttmeir. Ian smiled and said in his experience, it was wise when dealing with upper management to defer the direction of the conversation to them, as they are more accustomed to being in control. Dr. Washington smiled and paraphrased the advice as the equivalent of "speak when spoken to." Anna, listening to the whole exchange, added that Elijah was going to experience a unique personality tomorrow, and she was sure he had encountered many similar situations. He assured her calmly that he was confident he would survive.

28

Do You Wake Up This Way Every Morning, or Do You Purposefully Have to Work Yourself into a Foul Mood?

A pessimist is a man who thinks everybody is as nasty as himself, and hates them for it.

—George Bernard Shaw

Dr. Washington walked down to the dining room early and told Cookie he needed whatever qualified as brain food, no matter how it tasted. Cookie reminded him that she never served anything that didn't taste wonderful, even the stuff that was healthy. She came back with a beautiful fluffy omelet, whole wheat toast with almond butter, and some beautiful green grapes. She explained these were three of the top-seven brain foods, and they paired well at breakfast. He nodded respectfully and settled in to finish the healthy feast in front of him. About twenty minutes later, he thanked Cookie and headed toward the reading and game room to spend a few minutes doing what calmed him the most, outside of swimming.

A few residents were playing cards, and a few more were reading. He asked quietly if anyone minded a quick song. He sat for just a moment and then softly broke into a song. The initial piano opening was melodic and almost hypnotic in both tempo and notes. He took his time working through the piece, about four minutes, and when he finished, he sat quietly, letting his breathing normalize. He got up and nodded at the audience, and one of the card players asked the name of the musical piece.

Elijah said, "It's called 'Clocks' by an English group called Coldplay, released in 2002. Did you like it?"

"Yes, very much. It's kind of a haunting melody, don't you think?" replied the resident.

Elijah smiled and agreed and headed out the door to the courtyard. Not seeing George anywhere, he headed down the vermiculite path toward the butterfly garden and found him looking into the habitat.

George turned and said, "I'm on baby watch the next few days, as this first batch of chrysalises are all close to opening. In fact, you are here to assist in the release of number one! It's magic, believe me. Come over here and offer your forefinger to the newborn monarch, and watch it acclimate to its new world."

Elijah did as instructed, and sure enough, the monarch climbed onto his outstretched finger from the screen house ceiling, and he gently backed up and held his hand to the sky. After about a minute of slow wing-flapping, it jumped off his finger and flew to one of the milkweed plants and sat happily on one of the orange-and-red blossoms.

George looked at Dr. Washington and said, "Isn't life beautiful, Elijah?"

Elijah clapped him on the shoulder and agreed that it was indeed and thanked him for sharing the moment. He checked his watch and saw that his interview was in about an hour.

The last stop he wanted to make was to sit briefly with Anna and receive any more insights she cared to impart. She was on her cell, but she waved him in to sit down.

"Hey, I'm totally supportive of buying it from them if it is as nice as it sounds. Delivery would be easy. Back it out of their dock and pull it into ours next door, and it's at least 50 percent less than buying new! Go for it, sport, and let me know how it turns out. Love you. Talk later," finished Anna. She turned to Dr. Washington and explained that their new neighbors at the lake in Kalamazoo had a really nice pontoon boat for sale with all the accessories. She then said she couldn't wait to tell Esther that the boat was waiting at the new house for her approval.

Turning to business, she told Elijah that he should be his usual forthcoming self and engage Bob in much the same way he would a colleague. She shared candidly, in her opinion, based on his medical background and now personal experience with Serenity Acres, that her boss was not going ask anything that Elijah couldn't handle. She told him they had reserved the exam room at the central nursing station for their meeting, and Dr. Washington quipped that he hoped Mr. Struttmeir didn't glove up before they got started. She chuckled and assured him he wasn't inclined to engage in that level of probing questions.

Elijah headed down to have another cup of coffee prior to the meeting, which would start in twenty minutes.

As he exited, Bonnie came into Anna's office and closed the door. She sat and then said, "This is unsolicited advice, boss, but since I won't be able to offer much going forward, hear me out." She reached into her jacket pocket and pulled out her trusty Olympus mini recorder, which she used for verbal notes and occasionally transcribing a meeting.

"When you sit down with Struttmeir to download his thoughts on his interview with Dr. Washington, stick it in top desk drawer, hit Record, and leave the drawer slightly open. If it was good and he states as much, terrific, and we can all move forward as planned. If it turns out as I think it might, it would be handy to have his true rationale for rejecting Elijah as a candidate. I will be happy to transcribe the session and make it available to you and no one else. Then you can decide how strongly you want to advocate for Elijah to lead us going forward. Just remember, young lady, that when you deal with a snake, it's best to keep it at a distance or to grab it right behind the head just to let it know who's in control."

Anna thought for just a moment and then asked Bonnie to show her how to start recording.

*

Bob arrived fifteen minutes late, telling Anna that traffic was awful exiting Chicago and he was anxious to get on with the interview. Since he hadn't been there physically in almost nine months, she thought he might like to visit with staff or at least stroll the complex. No, thanks, he informed her; he had a dinner to get back to in Chicago with his wife, Cherise, and their neighbors, who owned a very successful chain of tire stores in the western suburbs. Anna told him she understood (which she absolutely did all too well) and walked him down to the dining room to find Dr. Washington and set them up in the exam room. Elijah stood and buttoned the top button on his gray English bespoke suit and offered his hand to Bob, who took it and looked up in awe, fear, and obvious discomfort. Anna escorted them the short distance down the hall, made sure the room had water, and left them to it.

They faced off across a small square table, and Dr. Washington, following Ian MacDonald's advice, waited for Mr. Struttmeir to start the interview. Bob took out a small notebook from his briefcase, opened it, and then posed the first question.

"Well, Dr. Washington, your résumé and accomplishments span quite a bit of time and are very impressive. You've held a number of important roles. Why would you aspire to manage a small nursing home in rural Wisconsin?" he posed.

"Thanks for the compliment, and I will probably explain my interest in Serenity Acres and Silver Age Industries by referencing those things on my résumé. The last twenty years have found me spending more and more time further away from the actual enterprises with which I was affiliated. Board meetings, finance meetings, executive management sessions, and the like are all very interesting, but they deal with their various enterprises at the abstract or analytical level. In the case of the hospital, we were usually ten floors removed from the actual business of patient care, and in the case of a not-for-profit, we were tucked away in the executive suite and far removed from the art and the people who came to enjoy it. Only at my medical practice, which was reduced to one office day a week, was there a tactile feel to the work. Here, on the other hand, I am immersed with the residents, the staff, the contracted medical practitioners, and the everyday life and rhythm of the place. Simply put, it appeals to me in a way that work has not for quite some time. Does that make sense, Mr. Struttmeir?"

"I suppose it does. Do you think you have the energy to fulfill the daily and weekly requirements of the position? Many people at your age are looking to slow down and enjoy hobbies and the fruits of their labors," said Bob rather inelegantly.

Unfazed, Dr. Washington said, "I understand that it is a societal norm for mature folks to step back from whatever their work was at some point to smell the roses, so to speak. I also have seen the empty lives of some of my colleagues, who play four or five rounds of golf a week and are on a first-name basis with every maître d' in a five-mile radius of where they live. Honestly, that has no appeal to me, and I also think I have something left to contribute."

Bob simply nodded and looked at his notes. The next question was one that Elijah had hoped he would ask and was fully prepared for.

"Since you have spent the amount of time here you have, has anything come to your attention that might improve the care or environment, in your opinion?" asked Bob.

"In discussions with several of the staff members, a few things have surfaced that I think might be worthy of some exploration. Apparently, the number-one reason for missing work or having to leave prematurely during a shift is childcare. Many organizations are beginning to address the issue head-on by offering limited childcare services on-site. That might be worth exploring.

"Our two excellent nursing directors have begun to explore what they called a geri-gym, which would entail space and some specialized equipment to improve both strength and aerobic capacity. Fairly certain you could staff that with part-time contract PTs who would bill directly for Medicare services in much the same way our psychologist does. The upside would be improved stability and fewer falls with residents—which, as you know, is a constant issue in long-term-care settings. I think that idea deserves some thought as well. I must say that Anna has done such a good job of hiring, organizing, and managing that simply sustaining her efforts would be a worthy goal for whomever takes her place."

"OK. Those sound ambitious. Could you describe to me your management style in a few words?" asked Bob.

"Good question. I would call it a combination of those of all the people that I have worked for who were great managers. I would start with the concept of management by walking around, which here would be both informative and fun. Secondly, I believe strongly in empowerment, which is essentially allowing staff to make decisions—within reason—and learn from their own successes and mistakes. Then I would add goal setting of both an operational nature, which you could review quarterly, and a personal nature, which would be looked at annually at review time. There are more, but those are probably foundational to how I lead."

After about twenty more minutes of fairly elementary questions, Bob thanked Elijah and said he needed to wrap up with Anna and then head out. Elijah thanked him and thought that would amount to about two hours on-site after making a six-hour round trip to Hidden Falls. Interesting use of time.

29

This May Be the Last Time

The best revenge is to be unlike him who performed the injury.

—Marcus Aurelius

After about an hour, which seemed a little short given the importance of the meeting, Bob showed back up at Anna's office and seated himself without being asked to do so. *No surprise there*, thought Anna as she closed the door and returned to her desk, seated herself, and activated the recorder in her center drawer smoothly without looking down.

"Well, I had a feeling this idea was not a good one, and I'm not delighted that I had to drive six hours today to simply confirm that. Let me start by saying that he is probably one of ten black people in this entire county. Culturally, that means he is starting from a, shall we say, difficult position with the residents and staff as well. Secondly, his age a is real red flag. Someone in their midseventies should be playing with their grandchildren, brushing up on checkers, falling asleep with back issues of *Reader's Digest*, and enjoying time with others in the same boat. His lack of understanding of how a facility like this runs in a profitable manner was just sad. He had multiple ideas he wanted to institute immediately that would add tremendous cost with no proven benefit. He wants a full-time and free day care center for employees' children, he wants a custom-fitted old person's gym manned by a PT here at the facility, which apparently is the brainchild of your two lesbian nursing managers. Lastly, he talked about a management philosophy that involved wandering around the place, empowering people, and setting goals. I felt like I was in the presence of some New Age management consultant, not a legitimate candidate for administrator. To be honest, I am stupefied why both corporate HR and you think this was a good idea. It doesn't surprise me that this kind of harebrained idea would appeal to Kirsten, our esteemed COO. I know this isn't politically correct, but for me, it's the kind emotional and sentimental idea you get when an organization is overpopulated with women. It appears that leaving the task of filling your position under your management was a real mistake, and I will have to clean up the mess. Remind me again when your last day is, please."

Anna took a deep breath and immediately had a new appreciation for how wise Bonnie was. Then she told herself that if she told the piece of shit sitting in front of her right at this moment what she really thought of him that he would win. Her next statement was difficult but necessary.

"Gosh, Bob, I feel terrible to have disappointed you so thoroughly. My time here at Serenity Acres and Silver Age has been so rewarding, and I do so want to leave on a good note. What can I do in the next two weeks to assist you with the transition?"

"Well, for starters, you can call Med Find or Med Hunt or Med Whatever and put a fire under their ass to dig up a decent candidate. Then let me know what they come with, and I will do the screening. It seems like that is the only way this is going to get fixed."

He stood up, and Anna had one wonderful thought. *This is the very last time I am* ever *going to set eyes on this motherfucker*, and she smiled, saying, "I'll get right on it, boss!"

The consummate asshole turned and marched out of building, saying nothing to anyone on his way to his leased E-Class with the vanity plates.

Anna clicked off the recorder, rewound a bit, said a prayer, and hit Play. There, in all his eloquent bigotry, was old Bob explaining his rationale for rejecting Dr. Washington as a candidate as well as his views on a number of other subjects. She smiled, stopped the unit, and called for Bonnie to join her. Bonnie came in and sat down with her pen and pad and waited for Anna to share what had transpired.

Before she gave the rundown and talked about next steps, she said, "OK, partner. Tell me how you knew what I was going to hear and why it would be beneficial to have a record of the conversation."

Bonnie shrugged and then said, "The simple explanation is that I have lived and worked for a while in a world that has plenty of assholes. They are self-centered and have contempt for anyone or anything that doesn't serve their interests or appears more competent than they are—which, in many cases, is everyone. However, they're skilled at masking this for the most part, but given the chance, they will share their true colors when they believe they are with someone who is under their control and powerless to do anything about it. Pretty simple, really. Just a learned knowledge of the dark side of human nature, if you want to give Bob the courtesy of categorizing him as human."

"Well, thanks for the advice and having my back once again. Rather than going through the whole gory discussion, why don't you just transcribe me a hard copy and give it to me in a PDF and you can hear it for yourself? Then retain the actual audio in case I need that as well. I'll be interested in your reaction," said Anna.

Bonnie left to complete the task, and Anna sat alone for a minute and thought about how she should handle the situation. She knew several things for sure. Number one was that Dr. Elijah Washington belonged here leading Serenity Acres. Number two was that Bob Struttmeir did not deserve the job he had and that he should not be working for Silver Age. Number three was that Kirsten Stanley was a good and fair executive and could be trusted to do the right thing. Number four was that she wanted to hear Elijah's version of his meeting with Bob, just to confirm what she was pretty sure she already knew.

She found Dr. Washington sitting with 75 percent of the Vera Bradley Bridge Mafia in the reading and game room. He was sitting in for Sarah Wilson, who was in town for a beauty appointment. His bridge was rusty, but they were polite and not very serious about the game to begin with, which made it enjoyable. Anna borrowed him, and they went outside to a table in the shade, and she had him go through his recollection of the interview, which confirmed her suspicions. Dr. Washington, being the gentleman that he was, told her that if this didn't work out, he would understand and still be around to volunteer at

Serenity Acres. She reached across the table and grabbed his hand and asked him if he trusted her. He stated that he did implicitly. She smiled and told him to stay tuned, winked, and went back to her office.

Bonnie had delivered the PDF to her e-mail in-box and on the way into the office asked her respectfully what she planned to do. Anna asked her in return how one dealt with a bully. Bonnie ventured that one socked them in the nose. Anna said that in this case, one got a running start and kicked them square in the balls as hard as one could, at which time she walked to her office and closed the door, asking not to be disturbed for a while.

She thought about her next move and felt good that her primary objective of leaving Serenity Acres in the very best hands possible would be well served by what she had planned next.

30

And the Truth Will Set You Free

If you're really a mean person, you're going to come back as a fly and eat poop.

—Kurt Cobain

Anna made some talking points and reviewed them to help her organize her anticipated conversation with Kirsten Stanley. She knew intuitively that this was a time-sensitive issue for a number of reasons. Her exit was imminent, Bob was capable of any number of outlandish claims, and Elijah was patient but, like anybody, expected a prompt and reasoned response. So she picked up her landline and dialed Kirsten's office number. Kirsten's administrative assistant answered and said Kirsten was in a meeting with the VP of HR in her office. Respectfully, Anna said she thought what she wanted to discuss with Kirsten was something she wouldn't mind being interrupted for. The administrative assistant asked her to hold.

Fifteen seconds later, she came back on and said she would put Anna right through to Kirsten's office. Kirsten answered by asking how the interview with Dr. Washington had gone. What she heard next fell into both the shocking and dismaying category. Anna gave her the essential overview of the morning, including Dr. Washington's interview, his description of the meeting, and Bob's download on the interview to Anna. Kirsten stated that she was certain what Anna had shared of his remarks to her were true but feared that it could turn quickly into a classic "he said, she said" situation. Anna delivered the next piece carefully.

"I was anticipating the same thing based on my past experience with Mr. Struttmeir and therefore recorded the session. I have a complete transcription on a PDF and of course have retained the audio recording itself. Would you like me to send the PDF to you?" asked Anna.

After a moment of what Anna assumed was shocked silence, Kirsten instructed, "Yes, send it to me via company e-mail and marked *Confidential.* Keep the original audio recording safe and intact at your office, and give me forty-five minutes to review the transcription and call me back. Know that I will most likely share it with our VP of HR."

"Yes, ma'am," replied Anna, and she hung up and set about constructing and sending off the e-mail.

*

Exactly forty-five minutes later, Anna called Kirsten back. The conversation started with an apology.

"Anna, let me start out by saying that I am truly sorry for someone in our employ to have not only said these things but subjected you to what I'm confident is his style of discourse and management for multiple years. Help me work through this, and I promise you the company will be most appreciative."

"Kirsten, as I have stated before, my concern is not with how I have been managed or spoken to but that my facility, residents, and staff are given an administrator that they deserve. *Competent* and *caring* are the two things at the top of my list. I thought we had found someone that was a great fit, and I still believe that. If that's where this is headed, I will run through a wall to help you get it done," said Anna.

"We'll run through the walls for you, Anna—you have my word. Oddly enough, I was talking to our CEO and VP of HR about another opening this morning before you called. It seems that Dr. Homer Lattimore, the current medical member of our board, which our company rules require, is leaving due to some health issues. David Milligan, our CEO, asked if our candidate for Serenity Acres might have board and medical oversight experience, and if so, might he be interested in filling both jobs. Here's what I'm thinking. I will send you a first-class ticket for Dr. Washington to fly to Philly on Monday from O'Hare. We will have a car waiting for him at the Philly airport. You limo him or whatever it takes on the outgoing and the return from Hidden Falls. We will have a room for him on Monday night at the best hotel in King of Prussia, and David and I will take him to dinner. In the meantime, I will be working through the issues we have with Mr. Struttmeir, and you don't have to deal with him—you have my word. Can you help us with this, please, Anna?"

"Just what I was hoping to hear, and we will have the candidate there on Monday, Kirsten. If this is my last involvement with Silver Age, it will be a fitting end to a wonderful five years. Thank you from the bottom of my heart," finished Anna.

Anna walked out to share her call and the outcome with her partner in crime, Bonnie, who hugged her mightily and gave a bit of a shriek. Then she took off on foot to hunt down Elijah and tell him he needed to pack for a quick trip to Silver Age headquarters on Monday to meet with the COO and CEO. He started to probe as anyone would, and Anna assured him it was all good stuff and that he had trusted her to this point and needed to just a bit longer. Then she got the best news of the day. Tom had indeed purchased the cool pontoon from the new neighbors and was headed home as they spoke and would be there in time to take her and the girls out to dinner. This day was going to end much better than it had started.

31

These Are a Few of My Favorite Things

The best good deeds are the ones that are performed quietly.

—Anonymous

Saturday started for Elijah in much the same way a lot of days at Serenity Acres did. Before breakfast and with a cup of coffee in hand, he had walked down to Edgar's room, pulled the side chair up to his bed, and talked about his week and the plans for the day. He told Edgar there was a chance he would be at Serenity Acres in an official capacity going forward, and he hoped that came to pass. He shared with him the outing that was planned for the day and where they were headed, with genuine excitement in his voice. Lastly, he asked him if there was anything he needed, knowing that he wouldn't get a response but also confident it mattered that if Edgar heard him, he would know he had a friend nearby.

After joining those who were taking the excursion for a light breakfast in the dining room (Emmaline, Sarah, Suzanne, Verna, June, and George), Dr. Washington excused himself and went off in a quiet corner to call Anna. She picked up and told him she was making pancakes and bacon for the three sleepyheads who had yet to make it downstairs. He laughed and told her that he couldn't remember if he had thanked her for everything she had done for him and that he needed to remedy that if he hadn't. She assured Elijah that his presence at Serenity Acres was more than enough to pay back any small thing she might have done for him and that that was what friends were for. Dr. Washington thanked her anyway and then before hanging up told her they were not friends as far as he was concerned; they were family.

Elijah met the others in the lobby, where Emmaline was on the phone making arrangements for lunch. She turned to them and said, "One of the company vans is almost here, and we will be on our way shortly. Will and his wife, Carrie, will be hosting us for lunch at their home—my former residence—and I think it will be a lovely day! I hope you all are ready to taste some cheddar."

Three minutes later, the big white fifteen-passenger Ford van pulled up out front with *Yoder Farms* emblazoned in green on the side, and off they went for the fifteen-minute ride to the Yoder Wisconsin Cheddar plant on the other side of Hidden Falls. The plant was situated on thirty acres of flat land just outside of Hidden Falls and was owned by the family, along with several thousand more acres in the county.

As they were making the short trip, George leaned over to Elijah in the back row of seats that they had volunteered to take, and in his seldom-used inside voice, he whispered, "Hey, Doc, just a word to the wise. I did the tour three years ago, and it is really fascinating. At the end, they take you to the tasting room, and you sample all the different types of cheddar they produce, which are all wonderful. Without thinking, I must have had damn near a pound and a half of cheese during that session, and I didn't shit again until the following week. Take small pieces of each type, no matter how much they offer."

Elijah smiled broadly and said, "Thanks for the tip, my friend. Will do."

*

George was absolutely correct on all counts. The tour of the 120,000-square-foot Yoder Wisconsin Cheddar plant was indeed fascinating. Between the offices and the production space, there were approximately two hundred employees working two production shifts and producing millions of pounds of cheddar annually. The tour started in the receiving area, where the raw milk product was delivered and then transferred into gigantic holding tanks for ripening. Then the natural rennet was added in smaller vats and the temperature closely controlled to set the curds. Then the curds were cut, cooked, and drained, allowing most of the whey to be removed. At that point, the cheddaring process could commence, which involved setting, cutting, stacking, and ultimately milling the curds. Once those steps were accomplished, the salting took place, which removed more of the whey, lowered the moisture content, and added flavor to the cheese. The packing and pressing then took place and the cheddar would be aged for several months or as long as twelve years, depending on the type of cheddar being made. All this was overseen by Emmaline's youngest son, Ethan, who was the president of Yoder Wisconsin Cheddar Company and had taken time to lead the tour. Emmaline had proudly told the group that he had gone to the U in Madison and studied business before coming to work in the family enterprise more than twenty years earlier. The last stop was in the infamous tasting room, where George kept a close watch on Elijah as he sampled the delicious types of cheddar, thus ensuring his gastrointestinal health.

They departed the plant and headed another five miles or so north on a county road until they came to an impressive set of gates that led up a long driveway to a very large and well-preserved Victorian house painted pale yellow. A handsome middle-aged man and his wife waited on the huge wraparound front porch and descended the stairs as the van pulled up. Emmaline introduced her eldest son, Will, and his wife, Carrie, who ushered the group up to a gigantic table that had been set for lunch with pitchers of iced tea, lemonade, and fresh flowers. They all arranged themselves with Elijah purposefully seated next to Will at the far end of the table.

"Quite a beautiful place you have here, Will, and thanks for hosting us for lunch," stated Elijah.

"Glad to finally meet you, Dr. Washington. Momma has told us so many nice things about you, and may I offer my condolences for the recent passing of your wife."

"Call me Elijah, if you would, Will, and my stay at Serenity Acres with your mother and her wonderful group of friends has helped to put me back on my feet in short order. Tell me a little about yourself and the family farm you run, if you don't mind."

"Well, Elijah, I have my two wonderful parents to thank for everything you see around you here. The dairy farm we run is just over two thousand acres, which equates roughly to a piece of land that is a square with three-mile borders. We have a dairy cow herd of just over five hundred Holsteins and a staff of twenty-five. The main barn and production facility are about a mile north of the main house here, and the staff quarters are a quarter mile west of there. We provide housing and wages that keep our staff turnover way below the industry average, plus we shuttle our kids back and forth to school in Hidden Falls every day. Those are all things my parents instituted long ago. They sent me off to the U in Madison for school to major in animal husbandry, so we run a pretty modern, safe, and healthy operation. You have to work it hard every day, but I'd be lying if I said we don't make a pretty good living here. My mom and dad, God rest his soul, are the two decentest people I will ever know, and I'm only trying to be about half as good, and if I make it, I figure that will be a good life."

With that, a young, attractive Hispanic girl brought out platters of sliced ham, potato salad, and greens beans. Will introduced Maria, and when she had gone back inside, he told Elijah with pride that she was his foreman's daughter, home from college for the summer, courtesy of a scholarship from the Yoder Foundation.

What a wonderful family, thought Dr. Washington.

32

If the Head of the Fish Is Good, Shouldn't the Body Be Healthy, Too?

Don't judge a man by his opinions, but what his opinions have made of him.

—Georg Christoph Lichtenberg

With a direct American Airlines flight leaving at 8:50 from O'Hare, Dr. Washington was up at 3:30 and leaving Hidden Falls by 4:00 a.m. to ensure arrival in time to clear security. Anna had apologized for the early departure, but Elijah had laughed and assured her that men his age were used to getting up at all hours. The Lincoln sedan the livery used had a spacious back seat, and mercifully, the driver had asked what kind of music he liked, found a jazz station, and headed south without any chitchat. Courtesy of Angela and Toby, the Steinway, the leather sectional, his desk, the eight Charles Alston original works, and his entire wardrobe were all packed and at a moving company waiting to make the trip north. He had negotiated a lease / purchase agreement with the owner of the loft space that allowed him to make improvements with the understanding they would remain if he chose not to purchase the property. Dr. MacDonald had recommended a local custom builder who had done some updates on their craftsman cottage to design and build out what Elijah wanted, which would only take about four weeks. In the meantime, he would continue to enjoy Cookie's cuisine and the company of friends. He sat back and enjoyed the restful ride to the airport.

On the other end, Kirsten Stanley and David Milligan, CEO of Silver Age, were having a quick breakfast meeting in King of Prussia to review the day and plan moving forward. Kirsten once again assured David that she had covered the legality of the tape Anna had made of her conversation with Struttmeir with their general counsel. He had assured her that Wisconsin, like most states, was a one-party-consent state, which meant exactly what it said; a recording is legal if only one party consents and is aware it is being made, which is logically the person making the recording. That meant that the transcript and most importantly the captured audio were usable for them to make reasonable personnel decisions. David also wanted to explore how good or bad they were at Silver Age at providing channels for all level of employees to report inappropriate or abusive behavior by management, which validated Kirsten's high opinion of him as a leader. David had made a fairly early dinner reservation at the Capital Grille in King of Prussia because they had decent steaks and seafood and an above-average wine list. Plus, having been to Chicago multiple times with its myriad of great eateries, he was confident they were not going to impress Dr. Washington with food.

Kirsten came immediately to their small but impressive lobby to welcome Dr. Washington and took him through the HR department at the request of the VP, who wanted to get a look at "the guy with the killer résumé" and great personality. Kirsten shared this with him as they made their way to her corner office. He replied, "No matter how long you live, it's always nice to hear you've made a good impression."

They sat, and Kirsten asked him to give her the highlights of his long and distinguished career. She could tell that his time in actually practicing medicine had been the high point for him, and that explained why managing a long-term care facility had such appeal. He painted a picture of Serenity Acres that made her burst with pride and almost tear up: motivated staff, engaged and satisfied residents, vibrant social activities, and respected by all in Hidden Falls and surrounding areas. Lastly, he reinforced what she had known for some time: Anna Halstead was a superstar administrator who had created and nurtured the environment at the facility with skill, energy, care, innovation, love, and humor.

She asked what it would be like following her in that role.

He responded, "Fortunate." He then asked her if it was normal for her to interview administrator hires, and she said it was not.

Kirsten said, "Anna was not pleased with the feedback she got from Bob Struttmeir on his interview with you, and it was completely counter to our human resources' feedback and her experience. I listened and agreed with her, and at the same time, our CEO, David Milligan, had an additional thought about your involvement with Silver Age in another capacity, which I will let him present. So here you are at world headquarters enjoying our company!"

"Indeed I am, and I greatly appreciate the first-class flight and treatment you have afforded. Unnecessary, but fully appreciated," offered Elijah.

They headed for David's larger corner office, and after the introductions were made, and as she was leaving, Kirsten said she would see them later for dinner.

David Milligan offered Dr. Washington a seat in a club chair around a large coffee table and took one himself. "So tell me, Elijah, how was your trip thus far?" asked David.

"My trip, as I told Kirsten, has been most comfortable," said Elijah.

"Well, we are glad you are here, and I have to confess that my interest in you certainly involves our facility in Hidden Falls but also extends beyond that. In reviewing your impressive résumé, I noticed your extensive board-level experience with health-care organizations and not-for-profits over the years. It just so happens that Silver Age is losing the medical member of our board due to health reasons, I'm sorry to say. I have never been good at beating around the bush, so what I would like to talk to you about is the opportunity this opening creates for you to join our board as well as manage our award-winning facility in Hidden Falls.

"As you know, board work is much more intermittent in demands, and we believe that someone with your knowledge and energy could certainly handle both roles. Our corporate charter mandates that the board must have at least one physician member, and you, quite honestly, are the ideal candidate. It also occurs to me that having someone not only familiar with the operational challenges of running a facility but also hip deep in doing it would keep the rest of us board members grounded. So what do you think, Elijah? Could you play more than one position for us at here at Silver Age?"

"I think that sounds like a wonderful opportunity, David, and given the chance, I'd jump at it. I don't like beating around the bush much either." Elijah smiled.

David stood and clapped his hands together and said, "Well, then, let's get two offer letters together down the hall in HR and seal the deal this evening over dinner. What say you?"

"Lead on, Mr. Milligan, sir!" responded Dr. Washington, feeling much the same way he had when he'd landed his first choice for residency back in the 1970s.

*

Dinner at the Capital Grille turned out to be a great choice, and David was so excited, he had invited his wife to join the group because he really wanted her to meet Elijah. The evening was helped along with several bottles of Dunn Vineyard's Howell Mountain cabernet, and the first toast made was by Kirsten to Anna Halstead, who really made the whole thing possible. Elijah broke his one-glass rule and enjoyed himself as if he had spent the evening with close friends, which indeed he had.

33

Sometimes You End Up Somewhere Surprising

Being a parent is dirty and scary and beautiful and hard and miraculous and exhausting and thankless and joyful and frustrating all at once. It's everything.

—Jill Smokler, *Confessions of a Scary Mommy*

It was Tuesday midmorning, and Elijah was on his way back from King of Prussia in the same Lincoln sedan with the same driver listening to the same jazz station. He was in as good a mood as he could remember in the last several years. Given the depressive state he was in following Sandra's death, he felt it was nothing short of miraculous that he could feel this happy. This apparently validated that work he liked and took joy from was still very important to him.

About halfway back to Hidden Falls, his cell rang, and he saw that it was Angela. He answered immediately.

"Hi, sweetheart! How is your day going at the MASH unit?" joked Elijah.

"Good description, Dad, and it is going like any other day here. Busy, bloody, chaotic, exciting, and filled with mostly good outcomes. But that's not why I called. How was *your* day yesterday, young man?"

"Well, if this isn't the ultimate role reversal. Father reporting on how his employment prospects are shaping up to daughter. The answer is: fantastic. I accepted two positions with Silver Age. The main one is, of course, the administrator role at Serenity Acres, which I am so excited about. But get this! They also want me to join the board of Silver Age as the medical member. It meets quarterly in King of Prussia, and I negotiated the same travel package I am enjoying now as part of the deal. Life is, as they say, good! How about you and Tobias? Everything copacetic?"

"Actually, there are a few newsworthy items on this end. First one involves a wedding we are planning for three weeks from now at the house in Oak Park. Just a small family-and–close friend gathering for which we hope you can find room on your busy calendar. Secondly, we have begun to remodel the small guest bedroom upstairs at Oak Park into a nursery. Other than that, everything else is business as usual."

Dr. Washington asked the driver to pull over somewhere and told Angela to hold on just a moment. There was a rest stop just ahead, and the driver smoothly exited and pulled into the passenger car lot up by the picnic tables and the restroom. Elijah thanked him, exited the car, and went and sat on top of one of the picnic tables.

"Now I can respond appropriately!" stated Elijah with tears starting to find their way down both his cheeks. "I am so, so happy! I only wish your mother were here to enjoy the moment with us. I can't pretend to be totally surprised. Toby called me on Sunday and asked for permission to ask you. My response was something like "Hell yes, son! Get to it!" Now you tell me that I'm not only getting a fine new son-in-law but my first grandchild as well. Not to sound too biblical, but my cup has indeed runneth over. I have a wet handkerchief to prove it. Talk to me, young lady."

"Well, Dad, we decided my biological clock was fast at work and that we both wanted at least one child. Apparently, I am one fertile woman. Anyway, I am delighted these surprises both fall into the plus column for you. And I have thought a lot about Mom as Toby and I have grown close as well. While I am not particularly religious, I am confident that she knows about this and is just as pleased as you are. Anyway, I have to get back after it here, but let's talk soon so we talk make plans for the ceremony and reception."

Dr. Washington wiped his eyes and walked slowly back to the car, where the driver opened the door and asked him if everything was OK. Elijah told him it wasn't just OK, it was wonderful, and he thanked him for asking.

Back in the car, Elijah kept his cell out, went to his recent calls, and clicked on Toby's number. Toby picked right up, like any respectful soon-to-be son-in-law would. Dr. Washington, after telling him how profoundly happy he was with the news about the wedding and the baby, asked him for a favor.

"Toby, would you mind terribly this week, when you have time, taking my Bimmer over to Perillo BMW? I will contact the general manager and tell him to expect you. I'm going to sell it to him and buy a new four-wheel-drive pickup here in Hidden Falls. Suits my new neighborhood and needs better."

"Not a problem, Elijah. I wanted to put my new MKX in the garage anyway, and this will make that possible. Thanks so much for the kind words, and I look forward to talking soon. My mom and dad are very excited about meeting you in three weeks."

34

This Isn't a Shoe That's Going to Drop, Son, It's a Boot

Is fate getting what you deserve, or deserving what you get?

—Jodi Picoult

Kirsten Stanley and Susan Scanlon were headed out to Chicago bright and early on Wednesday morning. Kirsten had called Anna and told her immediately about the outcome of their meeting and dinner with Dr. Washington on Tuesday morning. She had instructed Anna not to take any calls or return any type of correspondence from Bob Struttmeir until she spoke with her the next day. She also told her that she would be in Chicago handling some personnel issues, and Anna was quick enough not inquire what those might be. Kirsten had notified Bob that she would be in Chicago on Wednesday and wanted to meet with him at the Silver Age regional office in Des Plaines at 11:00 a.m. on Wednesday. He had nervously agreed and asked what the meeting was about. Kirsten told him he would find out tomorrow at the meeting and hung up abruptly.

So at 10:00 a.m., Kirsten and Susan were exiting the United terminal at O'Hare and making their way to the cabstand. After giving the Kazakh cab driver the address in Des Plaines, Susan asked Kirsten if there was anything she needed from her during the meeting other than providing the separation agreement.

Kirsten remarked, "No, thanks, Susan. Just give me the separation agreement when I ask for it, stop me if I look like I am about to strangle this prick, and promise me that we will figure out ways to find these types of people before they do any of our employees or residents harm going forward."

They pulled up in front of the nondescript office building in Des Plaines twenty minutes later and were about twenty-five minutes early. Kirsten led them into the Starbucks on the first floor and bought two coffees. They rode the elevator up to the third floor and walked the short distance down the hall to office number 310 with the Silver Age logo on the plaque outside the door. They entered, and the receptionist smiled and said Mr. Struttmeir was expecting them and would be right out. Bob emerged twenty seconds later looking like he had suffered through a sleepless night. Kirsten said they would meet in his office and told the receptionist not to disturb the meeting.

After entering the office, Kirsten asked Bob if he had any idea why they were there, and he said softly he did not, but because Susan was there, he assumed it had something to do with a personnel issue. Kirsten said that it did and then commenced to explain. She outlined her understanding of his interview with Dr. Washington and then asked if he recalled his meeting afterward with Anna Halstead, in which he outlined his opinions on the candidate and other subjects. He said he had taken notes during the interview and that he had a vague recollection of his conversation with Anna. Kirsten smiled slightly, opened the file in front of her, and said, "Let me help you with your recollection of that meeting, Mr. Struttmeir. Here is a copy of a transcription of the meeting made from an audio recording. Take your time and read the transcript."

Bob slowly slid the two double-spaced typewritten pages in front of him and began the painful process of reading his and Anna's exchange. He felt no shame in his captured comments. In fact, he thought he had made some great points. Well, maybe the comment about the organization being "overpopulated with women," given the current audience, was not particularly well advised. But what about recording him without his consent? *That can't be legal,* he thought. So after he finished, he leaned back, put his hands behind his head, and said he thought his rights may have been violated.

Kirsten had spent enough time with Mr. Struttmeir, so she calmly went into a completely extemporaneous summation. "Well, your rights have not been violated, and if you take the time to consult counsel, which I am sure you will, you will hear that Wisconsin is what is termed a one-party-consent state. Simply put, the one party in this case was the one doing the recording. Now let me tell you what in fact has been violated. Your remarks clearly demonstrate misogyny, racism, homophobia, a comfortable relationship with lying, and last but perhaps the most offensive, ageism.

"Let me explain ageism to you, Bob. It is the stereotyping of and discrimination against individuals or groups on the basis of their age. While all those other demonstrated ugly traits would probably call to question your continued employment here at Silver Age, ageism is just a nonstarter given that we all make a living serving those who are older. So now Susan will provide you with a separation agreement, which you can read and sign now or take it with you for review by yourself or counsel. Either way, as of right now, you are no longer an employee of

Silver Age, and your computer access to the company system has been disabled. I will need your office keys now as you exit the building."

She stood and held out her hand. He looked and raised his palms to demonstrate he didn't understand.

"Your keys, Bob, now," said Kirsten without moving.

Bob slowly took out his key ring, removed the office key, and handed it to her, saying, "You will regret this, and Milligan will hear from me."

"The only thing I regret, Bob, is not doing it sooner. Now leave or I will have you forcibly removed."

He turned, grabbed his coat, and was gone in ten seconds without saying a word to the receptionist or the other regional employee, Claudia Herald, the controller of the Upper Midwest Region of Silver Age Industries. Kirsten said something to Susan, who went into the small lobby to speak with the receptionist while Kirsten invited Claudia into Bob's office.

Claudia sat down and looked wide-eyed at Kirsten with a mixture of awe and fear. Kirsten smiled and told her to take a deep breath and to let her explain what had just happened. Without totally impugning Bob's character, she said that the company had chosen to let him go for very good reasons. She then told Claudia that Silver Age really appreciated her work and that she had been instrumental in the financial health and results of the Upper Midwest Region.

Claudia breathed quite a bit easier and patiently answered some background questions that Kirsten posed—where she lived, how she liked her job, who her favorite administrators were, and if she was tied to Chicago. Claudia answered them all, and to the last one, she said that while she was a Chicago native, the traffic and cost of rent were both downsides. Kirsten said she understood and then asked Claudia if she trusted her. Claudia smiled shyly and said she not only trusted her but greatly admired her.

Kirsten told her that was great to hear and that for the short term she would report directly to her and they would talk daily. Kirsten stood, as did Claudia, and gave her a big hug. She thought, *My work here is done, and I need a glass of wine at the United Club Lounge at O'Hare.* She could call David with an update from there.

35

Giving Credit Where Credit Is Due

Mediocrity knows nothing higher than itself; but talent instantly recognizes genius.

—Arthur Conan Doyle, *The Valley of Fear*

The committee to recognize and celebrate Anna Halstead's time at Serenity Acres and in Hidden Falls was an intimate group of about 150 people. It was comprised of the staff, some of whom had worked for her during her entire tenure at the facility. It included local friends, neighbors, and businesses who had known Anna and her family as some of the best Hidden Falls had to offer. Last but not least, it included the residents of Serenity Acres, who had been the primary focus for her for just about 12,500 hours during her time there, and each and every one of them knew through their own experience just what that had meant. Friday, her last day and a day before her departure to the Halstead's new home in Kalamazoo, would be a celebration to remember.

Lunch was going to be an inside/outside affair with burgers, hot dogs, chicken, and corn cooked in the courtyard on a gigantic smoker grill rented for the occasion. Cookie was busy with big quantities of all the sides and salads that tasted and smelled like summer in Wisconsin. The long buffet in the dining room looked like the farmers' market held on the square every Saturday during the summer. The vendors that Anna had bought from for almost five years were all anxious to participate and had delivered their goods to Cookie on Thursday afternoon. She and the staff had come in at 4:30 on Friday morning and turned all the fresh goods into scrumptious dishes. The event was scheduled to start at noon, and in the meantime, the rest of the staff and residents watched with a sense of anticipation and melancholy as the preparations continued through the morning.

Anna had promised herself she would focus on all the wonderful times she had enjoyed with these great people and not to get the least bit maudlin. That was going to be hard, but she would give it her best shot. Like almost every morning since arriving at Serenity Acres as the administrator, she greeted her valued jack-of-all-trades, Bonnie, with a big smile.

Bonnie grabbed her travel mug half-full of Peet's Dark Roast House Blend and took it down to Cookie to top it off. She returned not more than two minutes later, handed it back, and said, "OK, boss, time for one last walkabout. Go see your people before the crowds from town descend on the buffet." She handed her the mug, put her thumb and forefinger to the corners of her mouth, and pushed it into a smile and shoved her on her way.

Anna's first stop was at the central nursing station, where the staff was assembled for a stand-up meeting with Melanie and Samantha. They all turned as she walked up and applauded quietly so as not to disturb the late sleepers and room-bound residents at the intersection of the two wings. She took her time and shook hands and hugged each of the ten or so care staff assembled.

Lastly, she came to Melanie and Samantha and said very gravely, "The one thing I want to share with both of you is that the toilet in the master bedroom has a tendency to run a long time occasionally. If you jiggle the handle, it stops. Pretty sure it's the mechanism in the tank. Tom was always going to fix it, but his intentions were hampered by his plumbing skills and his love of procrastination. There, I've come clean and can move on without regret." They both laughed hysterically and hugged her, which started to turn to a whimper party until she held them at arm's length and said, "Don't start, goddamn it! I'm going to make it through this day with nothing but smiles and laughs. Work with me here, girls."

They both wiped their noses and eyes and sent her on her way.

In the dining room, the four-seater next to the french doors, which had hosted so many important meetings and meals, was occupied by the Vera Bradley Bridge Mafia. Emmaline, Suzanne, Sarah, and Verna were locked in an intense conversation, and when they saw Anna walk in, Sarah waved her over to their table with a sense of purpose behind the gesture. Anna grinned broadly at the table and asked what they were discussing so earnestly.

Emmaline fielded the question. "Well, Anna, we could use your perspective on the subject under consideration. With your exit and Dr. Washington assuming the helm, so to speak, we are trying to determine just how 'trainable,' for lack of a better term, he might be. The points made were that he was a doctor by training and work, and to our experience, that group has a tendency to be quite full of themselves. Secondly, his multiple board positions indicate he must listen well and give good advice, which might be considered somewhat encouraging. Lastly, he was married for fifty-five years, which, without knowing his dearly departed wife, might lead one to speculate he had been thoroughly housebroken, which works in our favor. Does that about cover the discussion, ladies?" The other three nodded wordlessly.

"So since it's my last day, why don't you share with me your similar meeting about me five years ago when I was the newbie," said Anna innocently.

"Well, dear, we are older, and remembering verbatim what the content of that discussion was could be challenging. However, as I recall, we jointly agreed that you were young, seemingly smart, and, on surface, eager to please. Given the five-year tenure and the number of people expected today for your going-away party, it would seem that we in fact did a splendid job of training you, and to give credit where credit is due, you overachieved," Emmaline said with a straight face.

"Now I know why you are known around Hidden Falls as the 'Velvet Fist,'" said Anna as the entire table, including Emmaline, burst into laughter.

"You do know, don't you, how terribly we will miss you, Anna?" asked Suzanne.

"Sure I do, and it's mutual. See you characters later," replied Anna.

She looked out into the courtyard, and George was trimming up the roses and various plants in preparation for the celebration, and June was seated at an umbrella table nearby, wearing a big straw hat. As Anna approached, she could see George stopping his pruning and reaching into one of the multiple pockets on his gardener's vest and taking out a small ziplock bag of small, flat brown seeds. She greeted them both, and George handed her the bag and told her it contained milkweed seeds for her to plant in Kalamazoo to attract butterflies at their new house. She was delighted and asked how to plant them.

George responded matter-of-factly, "Well, you put them down about an inch and water them, for fuck's sake. Whoops! There I go again with the impulse control thing Doc told me about. And on your last day!"

"George, don't sweat it. It was kind of a dumb fucking question, anyway." Anna laughed.

June was standing next to George and patted his arm reassuringly and then said, "While we will miss you terribly, Anna, I have to thank you for bringing Dr. Washington here and then recommending him as the administrator. We will all be well served by that move, staff and residents alike."

Anna gave her a thumbs-up and headed back to her office to begin packing up her personal stuff, which Bonnie would help with. She gave Tom a call to check and see how the packing and loading of their household goods was going and told him she would have her beloved antique minivan there by late in the afternoon to pack it on the truck. He had tried to talk her into selling it and buying new in Kalamazoo, but she had steadfastly insisted it still had a few good years, and the vomit and crushed pretzel / animal cracker crumbs in all the deep holes in the carpet in front of the middle seat reminded her of her babies. He told her he would be there with the girls at lunch and they would all be hungry, so what was she cooking?

*

All the friends from Hidden Falls started arriving at around 11:45, and the cars overflowed onto the lawn. The crowd included the mayor, two county council members, ten neighbors with their kids in tow, Mildred, who owned the Nook, about ten members from the community hospital staff, and of course, Ian and Erin MacDonald. Others kept arriving after the buffet and barbecue grill were netting all kinds of goodies. Anna was particularly touched when the EMT who drove for the local ambulance service showed up. He bowed his head in deference and respect to the women who had tearfully accompanied every deceased patient from

Serenity Acres to the county morgue at the hospital for the last five years.

Anna was her usual gracious self, going out of her way to introduce Dr. Washington to all those in town who had yet to meet him, telling them how lucky Serenity Acres and Hidden Falls were to have landed such a man into their midst. Tom, Esther, and Melissa were having a great time with the neighbors and their children, with Melissa guiding Dr. Washington around to meet all her buds.

At around 3:30, Anna signaled Tom it was time to head home, and she kept a stiff upper lip as she walked out of the front entrance, with Bonnie helping by carrying the banker's box to the venerable van. Bonnie and Anna hugged, and without needing to say anything, Anna drove off one last time, and Bonnie went inside to help clean up from the boss's farewell party.

36

Moving Would Be Fun if You Didn't Have to Deal with All Your Stuff

The best way to not feel hopeless is to get up and do something. Don't wait for good things to happen to you. If you go out and make some good things happen, you will fill the world with hope, you will fill yourself with hope.

—Barack Obama

The most important thing that Anna could claim about the move was that they had all survived. The road trip on Saturday morning had started at 8:30 a.m., with a stop for lunch off I-94 as they crossed into Michigan at the cool little lake town of New Buffalo. They made it to the new house by late afternoon, in time for their very first pontoon ride. Both Esther and Melissa got to steer the boat with Dad's help, and just like the night before in Hidden Falls, they camped out on the floor in their sleeping bags, which explained her slightly achy back.

The movers arrived midmorning on Sunday, and they began the task of fitting all their stuff into their new digs, which were absolutely stunning. The great room / kitchen combination was lakeside, with a wall of glass looking out over their small lakeside lawn, their pier, and of course Gull Lake and its 2,300 acres. Sunday was spent with the movers' help setting everything in the right rooms. Monday and Tuesday had been unpacking and setting up each room. Now it was Wednesday morning, the girls were off to their new school, Tom was back at headquarters starting a new training class of Stryker sales recruits, and Anna was stretching in her sweatshirt and lounging pants at the end of the pier with a big cup of Peet's, admiring her new view. Her iPhone chimed in her pocket, and she held it up to see Kirsten appear via FaceTime in front of her.

"My, don't you look relaxed. I am very jealous, Anna! Where are you standing?" Kirsten said.

"On the end of our pier with a big cup of Peet's and a cluttered house behind me waiting for further organization from *moi*."

"Point the phone at the house. I want to see! Wow! Now I'm really jealous."

"So how are things with you?"

"They're pretty darn good and hopefully about to get better. Do you have a few minutes to talk right now?"

"Sure. Let me walk back inside and sit down at the breakfast counter in the kitchen. Could I just call you back? I'm really not ready to present my mug to the you or the world quite yet," said Anna.

"Yeah, that works fine. Why don't you give me five and call me back while I tell Midge not to disturb us," said Kirsten.

Curious, Anna clicked off and headed back up to the house.

After topping off her coffee, she dialed Kirsten back and sat looking out at her lovely new backyard as she waited to restart the conversation.

Kirsten picked up and said, "So I know that it's only been a couple of days for you to think about what's next, but if you don't mind my asking, What's next for Anna Halstead?"

Anna hesitated and then said, "Well, I have my résumé with Med List and have just begun to do some digging around locally in the hospital market here in Kalamazoo. Between the Bronson, Ascension, and Borgess systems, the emergency medicine side is fairly target rich, and my background and references in that segment are very strong. Candidly, with Tom's new job and salary, I have the luxury of not rushing into something just for the income, but I do want to go back to work." Then Anna relaxed and waited for the real reason for Kirsten's call to be revealed.

"It's great to be in that position; a lot of people in today's economy aren't afforded that luxury. Let me bounce something off you that during the course of our mutual ordeal involving Mr. Struttmeir and Dr. Washington made itself very clear to me and others here at Silver Age. You are an asset to anyone you work for. We have five years invested in you, and the arrangement has been a very good one for Silver Age. Both David and I would really like to find a way to keep you on board, and following your example, we have been involved with a little outside-the-box brainstorming. Prior to letting Mr. Struttmeir go, Susan Scanlon and I conducted a series of phone interviews with your former peers at all the Silver Age Upper Midwest Region facilities that Bob managed. After assurances, to a person, each of them described similar experiences with Mr. Struttmeir, and then Susan asked them who they went to for guidance and advice if they could not rely on their boss. Again, to a person, the first individual they mentioned was you. Whether it was a personnel, quality, medical, or general management issue, they were confident in getting good advice from you. Then last week, on what I'm sure Struttmeir remembers as 'Black Wednesday,' before we headed back to Philly, I sat down with Claudia Herald, the Silver Age regional controller, who also confirmed that you were, in her opinion, by far the best administrator in the Midwest. Then I asked her how she liked Chicago and if she would ever consider moving for the right opportunity, under the right boss in the right place. She said yes enthusiastically to all those things, which leads me to the following. Would you consider becoming the new VP of the Upper Midwest Region of Silver Age Industries and setting up a new regional office there in Kalamazoo? We would pay to move Claudia there and give her a housing allowance for the first twelve months. The offer to you would be slightly higher than what we were paying Mr. Struttmeir, which doubles your old salary. There would also be the standard stock option grant awarded to all VP-level personnel of one hundred thousand shares, vesting over four years. I will share with you that given our stock performance over the last few years under David's leadership, that benefit, for me personally, pretty much covers my retirement planning. So let me stop now and hear what your reaction is."

Sitting slack-mouthed and with moist cheeks, Anna regained her composure and said, "Well, I didn't see that coming! I took notes and think I was able record everything you went over in terms of the position. Just to process a few things out loud, if I were to take on the responsibility, the job would require some travel the way I would do it. Michigan, northern Indiana, northern Illinois, and central and southern Wisconsin are all drivable. Minnesota and northern Wisconsin would require air travel. Is there a company car and gas card, and would there be a reasonable travel budget to make sure I could manage and support the Upper Midwest as it should be? If the answer to those things is yes, I think after a conversation with Tom, the answer would most likely be yes."

Kirsten was absolutely ecstatic but worked hard at hiding her joy when she said, "I'm pretty sure the answers will be yes after I run it past David, and then we will e-mail you an official offer letter today. Could we expect an answer by Friday?"

"Kirsten, you'll have an answer later today. Can I hang up and call my husband, please?" asked Anna.

"You bet. Talk to you soon," replied Kirsten.

A moment later, Anna was on the phone calling Tom at work. The class was taking a break, and he picked up and asked if everything was OK. Anna restrained herself and asked if he remembered when he had interviewed for his new job here at Stryker and called her because he wanted to say yes immediately.

Tom said, "Of course I do, but what does that have to do with anything?"

She explained rapidly, and he only had one question.

"Do we have another bottle of Caymus cab?"

37

Is There Any Event More Fun Than a Wedding?

Weddings are important because they celebrate life and possibility.

—Anne Hathaway

The great thing about having a wedding in a private setting that you own is that you are playing by your own rules and by what your neighbors will agree to. The good news for the neighbors was that the attendees numbered only fifty, the music was provided by a string quartet and then a four-piece jazz ensemble, and the whole affair would wrap up by 10:00 p.m. at the very latest.

Angela was a longtime holder of season tickets for the Chicago Symphony Orchestra and called the membership director to ask if they had a performance the night of the wedding, asking to be put in contact with symphony members who moonlighted as string quartets for events. She received the list and chose a group headed by the first-chair violinist and the second-chair cellist. They had the set list (Vivaldi, Mozart, among others) and said all they required was the outline of the ceremony with musical interludes noted and a sizable check in advance.

Toby said the amount for the music was fine since they were getting a deal from the officiant; it was the Right Reverend Bradford Galloway Esq., Toby's father. When they had floated the idea past him, he said he would find out what Illinois law required, and one week later, he was ordained online by the American Fellowship Church for one year. Lydia, Toby's mother, much to Bradford's dismay, steadfastly refused to address him as *Reverend*, saying that she had known him way too long and believed in lightning.

Angela dictated the wedding party attire by stating that she would be wearing a Marchesa floral-print tulle tea-length dress.

Toby asked what that meant for him, and Angela was mercifully short in her instructions: "Mid-gray suit, white shirt, black tie, black laced shoes, and belt. Any questions, sport?"

He replied, "No, ma'am," leading her to believe once again she had found a trainable mate.

Perhaps the most fun they had was arranging the food. Angela asked Toby if he had ever been to Shaw's Crab House on Hubbard Street. He said no, and she booked a table and an appointment with the chef for the next night. On the way there, she explained that her parents had been taking her there since she needed a booster seat, and he would see why they needed to cater the wedding dinner.

They were seated, and while Toby's glass of chardonnay and Angela's water were delivered, the chef appeared at the table. Angela introduced her fiancé and then explained they were getting married at the house in Oak Brook and wanted him to take care of the catering. He nodded solemnly and asked only if she trusted him to do it right. She said that's why they were there. He asked what time they should be there to set up, and she responded that dinner was scheduled for 6:30 and to back it up from there. He leaned over, kissed her on the cheek, shook Toby's hand, and told them both it would be memorable.

Toby looked at her, and she said, "Have dinner first before you ask anything."

Toby ordered four courses, and two hours later, on the way out, he told her he understood her decision completely.

*

The day arrived, the tent for the dining was set up, and the seven tables of eight were set inside the tent, with seating for the ceremony faced the back raised patio. Shaw's took over the kitchen and set the bar up out by the tent, and by 4:30, they were ready to receive the guests.

The guest list was evenly divided between the bride's and groom's families and friends. On the bride's side, the who's who of the Chicago medical community, colleagues from Angela's work, and a few close friends were seated. On the groom's side, his architectural colleagues, who were awestruck by the house, his sister and her family, and some close friends from college were seated as well. Dr. Washington had brought a guest along, who Angela finally found out was Suzanne Richards Holmby, a friend from Hidden Falls who had been in the newspaper business. Elijah had reassured Angela that their friendship was strictly platonic, and they both intended to keep it that way.

At 5:30 on the button, Reverend Galloway stood on the top step of the patio and welcomed the attendees, and the quartet started with Mozart as Toby escorted his mother, Lydia, to the front row reserved space. Then Vivaldi commenced as Dr. Washington and Angela made their way to the front down the center aisle, and Elijah proudly offered her into the hands of her handsome husband-to-be. Bradford instructed the attendees like he might a jury that he had been given twenty minutes to complete the ceremony, and in he dove. His remarks were mildly humorous, filled with love and emotion for the couple and delivered with a deep bass that commanded attention. Exactly nineteen minutes into the ceremony, he looked at his son and said, "Well, don't just stand there, Tobias. Kiss your bride!" The crowd erupted in hoots and applause as the string quartet played them down the aisle toward the tent and thus the reception.

Elijah hustled to his friends from the jazz club, who were set up by the bar. He took off his coat, rolled up his sleeves, stepped behind the Yamaha portable keyboard, sat on the stool, looked at the trumpet, sax, and bass guitar players, and said, "Somebody needs to play something, boys. Lead us out, Cecil."

The bass guitar player laid down a couple of notes, and they were off on a soft jazz version of "That Old Black Magic," and Elijah chuckled at the irony. Bradford found his way to Elijah, slapped him on the back, and said it was too bad the kids were on such a tight budget they had to rely on family to defray the cost. Suzanne had found Anna and Tom and was inquiring about the girls, their school, the new place, and Tom's opinion about his wife's new position. Tom told her it was the best thing ever because she would be driving something from this decade now. Suzanne told her that she had been given explicit instructions by the crew at Serenity Acres to take her picture waving and bring it back, which she did.

The guests enjoyed their drinks and snacks while the staff from Shaw's was setting up the seafood buffet up on the patio by the kitchen. Toby dinged a wineglass and invited all to join them at their seats under the tent. He acknowledged his beautiful bride, his mom and dad, his sister and family, and Dr. Washington.

Promptly at 6:30, the head table walked up to the buffet, marveled at the spread, and dug in. When the last table had made their way back to the tent, Dr. Washington invited Reverend Galloway up to say grace, and he so did eloquently and briefly, which Elijah said was difficult for attorneys, drawing a good laugh. Then he toasted the happy couple, raised his glass to the air, and did the same silently to his wife of fifty-five years. *I need one of those corny T-shirts that says "Life Is Good." Do they make them in black with a stylish script that would go well with my Armani sport coat?*

38

Settling In

A journey of a thousand miles begins with a single step.

—Lao-Tzu

Dr. Washington was excited to start his new job on the Monday after Angela and Toby's wedding in Chicago. He had joined the Hidden Falls YMCA, and this was his first morning to swim before heading out to Serenity Acres. He helped open up at 6:00 a.m. and headed back to the spacious six-lane, twenty-five-yard-long lap pool at the Y. He joined one other person and took it nice and easy with alternating freestyle/breast fifties until he had put in just over thirty minutes. Although he was a little rusty from not having swum since before Sandra's death, the slight fatigue felt good as he climbed the steps out of the pool. He headed back to the loft, which had turned out quite well. The stairs up placed him into the kitchen / great room, and he turned on the Keurig before walking through the door to the master suite for a quick shower. The builder had overachieved in the master bath, and he felt like the star from *The Shape of Water* (minus the scales) as he stepped into the oversized glass shower enclosure. The master closet was just as impressive with twelve-foot pole hangers down one side with sport coats and suits on top and dress shirts on the bottom. The opposite twelve feet had shoe shelves and a nice set of drawers, which easily handled all the other clothes comprising his extensive wardrobe. Elijah was unapologetic about his love of clothes; he told his closest friends that it stemmed from his father's advice to always look his best. He put on his favorite navy blazer, a pair of gray tropical wool pants, and his cordovan Alden loafers and headed to the kitchen where he grabbed his travel mug and the Cinnabon coffee from the Keurig. He smiled as he remembered Sandra teasing him that he drank "girlie coffee," and he'd retorted that he was a man comfortable in his own skin.

He locked up, descended the stairs, and exited the back of the building to his reserved parking spot where his new Ford F-150 Limited Super Cab awaited. Angela had really gotten a kick out of his new vehicle and had asked playfully if he was going to get a cowboy hat and play Nat Love (a.k.a. Deadwood Dick) on the way to work every day. He often regretted sharing his infatuation with Nat Love as a boy with her when she was little, although he knew the lesson Nat represented was not lost on Angela. Her idol growing up was Dr. Joycelyn Elders.

Elijah enjoyed the short, picturesque ride out to Serenity Acres and proudly pulled into one of the staff spaces in the parking lot. It was 7:45 a.m., and the staff lot was already full with eight to ten cars. He walked through the front doors with his messenger bag and his travel cup and headed toward the office.

Bonnie was waiting for him. She took his travel cup and said, "Let me fill that up for you. Put your laptop on my desk, and I will get you set up on the Silver Age company network, including your new company e-mail address."

Elijah thought how lucky he was to have inherited not only Bonnie but the rest of the team. "Thanks, Bonnie. On the advice of my mentor and predecessor, I will start and complete my very first walkabout," said Dr. Washington happily.

"Great! Start at the nurses' station, and I will meet you there with your coffee," said Bonnie, already moving down the hall.

Dr. Washington chuckled at the seamless comfort of his first morning and headed as instructed toward the central nurses' station. As usual, the stand-up meeting was taking place with staff, and Elijah stood behind the group and listened as Samantha and Melanie discussed the importance of keeping contact notes current online for all patients. He was impressed, as this was difficult to accomplish with inpatient staff in his experience. They stopped and asked if he would like to say anything to the group, and he said how delighted he was to be there and that his door was always open for anyone who had questions about anything.

After chatting with the staff for a few minutes, he excused himself and headed down to the end of A wing to check on Edgar Vornoy. Edgar was resting in a slightly elevated position and stirred as Elijah entered and pulled up the chair to sit and chat. He took Edgar's hand and explained this was day one in his new role and that he was very pleased that he could continue to spend time with his friend. He asked if there was anything that Edgar needed and waited respectfully for the answer, which he was certain would not come. Then he squeezed Edgar's hand and got up and said he would see him the following day. Bonnie caught him with his coffee cup as he exited Edgar's room and told him breakfast was in full swing in the dining room. He thanked her and headed that way.

Walking into the dining room, he headed for the kitchen to see Cookie. She was stirring some oatmeal and smiled broadly as he approached.

"Good morning, Dr. Washington. And how are you on your first day here as our fearless leader?"

"I'm just super, Doreen, and you could help me out. Do you have a carafe of fresh coffee that I could take out into the dining room to freshen some residents' cups?" asked Elijah.

"Right over here; let me fill it for you," she said as she completed the task. "And when you are done doing that, please stop back here and let me fix you a plate to take back to your office. Breakfast is the most important meal of the day, and we can't have the chief running out of steam midday, can we?" added Cookie.

"Yes, ma'am. Make it two eggs over easy, two strips of bacon, and a piece of dry whole wheat toast. As Bogart said to Claude Rains in *Casablanca*, I think this is the beginning of a beautiful friendship."

Elijah walked over to the table by the french doors open to the courtyard and asked the Vera Bradley Bridge Mafia if he could freshen their cups. They smiled and said yes, thank you very much. As he moved away to repeat the offer to the other tables, Emmaline looked at the group and said that she had suspected that his acclimation might have been more of a challenge, but this obviously was a good start. Ten minutes later, after completing his rounds of the other tables, he exited the building and walked over to George, who was trimming the finished blooms off the rosebushes and putting the remains in a pail.

George looked up and said, "Hey! There's the new guy! Do you have time later today to head over to the nursery in town to pick up some bags of manure, mulch, and some burlap bags?"

Elijah smiled and said, "Sure, but won't that stink up my new truck bed?"

"Well, of course it will, you dumb shit! That's the whole point unless you want to drive that thing around town looking like the newbie. Oh crap, there I go again," lamented George.

Yup, I'm right where I need to be, thought Elijah as he walked back in to collect his breakfast.

Epilogue

Five Years Later

Serenity Acres

Dr. Elijah Roosevelt Washington is enjoying his fifth year at the facility immensely. They have instituted two new programs since his arrival (a geri-gym and an employee day care program) that have cut resident falls by 35 percent and unscheduled employee absence by 50 percent. Dr. Washington works a half day a week at Hidden Falls Family Practice, giving Dr. MacDonald a much-needed break as he oversees his original office and the new office in the Hidden Falls Community Hospital's attached medical office building. Dr. Washington has limited his board activity to his primary employer, Silver Age, and he is training to compete in the upcoming Senior Olympics hundred-meter freestyle at IU aquatics center in Indianapolis.

The Vera Bradley Bridge Mafia is reconfigured but still playing almost daily. Verna Winstadt passed away three years ago after a heart attack and is missed greatly. June
Wilhelm has stepped in and, according to Emmaline Yoder, shows promise but is unlikely to accumulate many master points. Suzanne Richards Holmby and Sarah Wilson are occupied with the *Hidden Falls Chronicle*, which a conglomerate bought and promptly run into the ground. It was purchased by Sarah Wilson and the Yoder Foundation with the understanding that Suzanne would be editor and would assure the paper would break even and most importantly serve the community of Hidden Falls.

Edgar Vornoy passed away shortly after Dr. Washington's arrival, and Dr. Washington arranged for a small portion of Edgar's ashes to be spread on the mound at the Wausau Woodchucks Field in Wausau by his daughter, Daphne, and her family, who will be forever grateful.

Bonnie and Doreen are running and feeding the place, respectively, and plan to do so as long as they are taking in air.

Melanie Grogan Smith and Samantha Smith Grogan are happily still running the medical aspects of the facility while enjoying their precocious four-year-old daughter, Anna. They are also planning a second child through the same intrauterine insemination process, but this time Melanie will be the vessel because her lower cervix really isn't that much shorter; she had "lost the toss" the first time.

Dr. Lipscombe is still happily contracted to provide psychological assessments and therapy while working closely with Dr. Washington and Dr. MacDonald along with the nursing staff.

Lastly and most sadly, George Binson suffered another stroke one year ago and did not survive despite heroic efforts by the facility and the Hidden Falls hospital staff. At George's service, Dr. Washington delivered a wonderful eulogy, promising to make at least one totally inappropriate comment per week. No eyes remained dry.

Silver Age Industries

David Milligan is still innovating away with the help of a marvelous board anchored by Dr. Washington. They are slowly and carefully implementing the geri-gym program and the employee day care model in all the other regions, with early signs that outcomes will be similar. David's favorite new toy is his new division, Alumni Aging Partners. It is set up to form joint ventures with major universities to develop near-campus housing for well-heeled alumni, with settings that progress from independent villas, to assisted housing, to full nursing-home care. The first ventures (Hoosier Hills outside Bloomington, Badger Meadows outside Madison, and Husker Highlands outside Lincoln) are nearing completion, and each are over 90 percent presold. The succession plan for Silver Age calls for David to take over the division full-time as it expands outside the Big Ten and goes national and for Kirsten Stanley to move into the CEO role, to which she has no objection.

Kirsten is very pleased with the expansion of her domain to include more than fifty newly acquired facilities that mirror demographically the secondary market model and payor mix of the original two hundred. She is particularly proud of the Upper Midwest Region under the management of Anna Halstead. It is now the number-one region and a model of clinical excellence and profitability that is the envy of not only her peers but the industry as a whole.

Anna will be the first to attribute that success to her regional controller and an amazing group of administrators, but they in turn will say they have the best boss in the company. Tom Halstead is now a VP at Stryker, which continues to innovate and lead the orthotics business nationally, and he can see himself retiring from there with one daughter going into the high school and the other entering middle school. Their beautiful lake property has risen almost 25 percent in value, with many homes now priced well above $1 million.

And last but certainly not least, Bob Struttmeir is divorced, which was Cherise's idea, and has a new career working for his neighbor at his Skokie location as the general manager of Big Dick's Tire, which fits him perfectly in so many ways.

The Rest of the Crew

The other Dr. Washington and her husband, Tobias Galloway, are both pursuing their respective careers and at the same time thoroughly enjoying raising the apple of both their eyes, Bradford Washington Galloway, who is four years old. Thanks to a rather long heritage of alumnae in the family and a history of generous donations, he has already been accepted at the Chicago Latin School. He is, at his father's encouragement, beginning a peewee-league basketball career, with the understanding that he will also be taking piano lessons soon under his mom's tutelage.

Although it has been a struggle, Angela left her role as medical director at the Northwestern Emergency Department and joined a prominent family practice group in Oak Park as a partner in order to more closely control her schedule. Tobias has just been made a full partner at his firm and is working on the firm's two largest projects. Their life is full, and they both feel blessed to have found each other and blessed with a child, all while holding down wonderful fulfilling careers. Life is indeed good.

Lastly, Dr. Robert Redfeather's time as president of the Ho-Chunk Nation of Wisconsin is coming to an end after two four-year terms. During his tenure, he fulfilled his primary objective of keeping the casino businesses operating very profitably and investing the proceeds in education, health care, and housing for his people. Homelessness among the Ho-Chunk people is virtually nonexistent, the primary health indicators for the members are all improving, and the high school graduation rates plus matriculation to college are now exceeding the comparable measures for the general population in Wisconsin. He has set his sights on the congressional seat that represents his home of Black River Falls and is blessed with a Republican opponent who is already characterizing him as a casino mogul with a drinking problem. He finds it amusing and has great faith in the people of his district recognizing his achievement as the president of his people in areas that they are indeed focused on: health care (Ho-Chunks have what amounts to universal coverage), education (improving results across all levels), and housing (where there is no homelessness). The upcoming debates will be fun.

While working on this book, I have had numerous people ask what prompted me to start such an endeavor. The reasons are many and varied, but there are several primary drivers. For those who know me well, I am not shy and love to express my opinions. Check out the *New York Times* comments section on articles for remarks by a sarcastic person from Southern California. Fiction is also a good forum to express opinions with and through the main characters who, for me, are conduits for how I feel about all sorts of things. I also have been fortunate enough to have had a long, interesting career in various for-profit health-care service companies, which has informed my writing and descriptions of the various aspects of health care explored in *The Best Home*. Lastly, I have the luxury of time to invest in writing, which has become the nearest thing to work for me.

The primary themes of the book are family, aging, race, and humor and how we are more alike than we are different. My experience in life is that wealth has little to do with happiness and that interesting people are more—than anything else—curious beings. The demographic shift in America has been dramatic over my lifetime.

Having grown up in a very racially diverse town in the Upper Midwest and attended a high school where, as a white person, I was a minority, my attitudes and opinions on race are grounded in overwhelmingly positive experiences as a child. My background in health care involved providing both products and services to a predominantly elderly population, whom I found interesting, smart, and engaging to a fault. Perhaps the most personal exposure to those of advanced age came from my mother, who lived to ninety-five, and my father-in-law, who reached ninety. These two individuals—born in 1915 and 1920, respectively—lived through epic periods of American history and in their own ways helped shape it. The Great Depression, World War II, the Cold War, and the civil rights movement were dynamic periods they participated in directly, and they were impacted by them.

Talking with them and being with them and in one case with their friends was always a rich, funny, and rewarding experience. I have always been drawn to older people, and I think it involves my curiosity with the times they experienced that I did not. I find the same curiosity in my children, who don't do much eye-rolling when my wife and I talk about our respective childhoods or our shared college experience.

Lastly, I have always been drawn to people who enjoy and use humor. Life is sometimes serious business, and to survive, there is nothing more beneficial than laughter. I have to admit that I share the offbeat and off-color humor demonstrated by some of the book's characters. Living is best done with a laugh and a glass of good cabernet, which is a subject I am interested in as well.

In writing this book, I drew exclusively on my own life experience and things I know. I hope it brings a smile to your face, reminds you of someplace or someone you once knew, and, if I really stretch, it stimulates you to write if you think you have a story in you. I'd like to read it.

Made in the USA
Las Vegas, NV
21 December 2020

14474982R10150